T0194915

MATTERS OF THE MOMENT

Malthouse African Fiction

MATTERS OF THE MOMENT

Tanure Ojaide

malthouse λ𝒫

Malthouse Press Limited

Lagos, Benin, Ibadan, Jos, Port-Harcourt, Zaria

Malthouse Press Limited
43 Onitana Street, Off Stadium Hotel Road,
Surulere, Lagos, Lagos State
E-mail: malthouse_press@yahoo.com
malthouselagos@gmail.com
Tel: +234 (01) -773 53 44; 0802 600 3203

© Tanure Ojaide 2009
First Published 2009
ISBN 978 978 8422 01 3

Distributors:
African Books Collective
Oxford, United Kingdom
Email: abc@africanbookscollective.com
Website: http://www.africanbookscollective.com

For:

my daughter, Eloho

1

She had been waiting for someone she had not seen. Many men in different costumes and habits had come to her as the one they wanted, but she knew that the right person had not come. She would recognize the man when she saw him, whatever the circumstances, she believed. She would make the person know that she had been waiting for him. That man had to be special and fortunate. She believed that things happened when they should. *Otie mr' ovwata, ko she-e,* she used to sing as a child in the village playground. When the ripe cherry fruit finds its favourite, it falls freely for the chosen one to pick.

She heard as soon as Dede returned, and imagined the eagle finally return to its nest on the crown of the *iroko* after extensively foraging the forest. The book farmer had returned home after completing his task overseas. The magician had arrived, she thought. Who, other than a magician, could speak the deep language of the ancestors long gone? she asked herself. She was yet to see him.

The stories about Dede, when he was abroad, were just too exciting for her. The elders fondly made fun of his childhood days when he used to recite poems he had studied at school in his dreams. From Dede's dream recitation of *Friends, Romans, and countrymen,* Uncle Tobi, now eighty-two, sitting in his cane chair and taking palm wine, still remembered and recited to his visitors in mangled English. Dede even sleepwalked, unaware of disasters on his way while speaking Latin that the old thought was the language of their ancestors. He was a bookworm with a photographic brain and always took the first position in his class, they recollected. Dede's relatives now living in Warri were not surprised that he went overseas to study because his type of

6

intelligence was the one that had taken many of their sons and daughters abroad to study law and medicine, favourite careers that landed one in wealth.

Franka eventually saw Dede at the party to welcome him from overseas after his graduate studies in public communication at Syracuse University. In Warri, such parties attracted the young and educated as corn left in the open did to parrots. They afforded the opportunity to meet many people and make new friends. The announcement of the party went out by word of mouth and spread fast; the party of the year. Although the invitation also was by word of mouth, those attending knew that the party was meant for them and they were expected to be there.

The welcome party was held at the spacious and elegant Lido Night Club in Ogedengbe Street, the most popular of its kind in town. Sitting cross-legged, Franka took a sip of Maltina with a straw. She chose not to drink from a glass. Now and then she raised the brown bottle and took a sip to wet her lips and tongue. Then she placed the bottle back on the table and wiped her lips with her tongue. She liked the cold dark drink whose savour left the aftertaste of honey. Beside her, a man was drinking Guinness Stout and cracking a chicken bone. Trays of fried goat-meat and chicken and other assortments of food and drinks were placed on tables before the seated guests. Also by the same table another man sat drinking Gulder beer, nodding his head to Sally Young's highlife music playing loud.

She had been keeping to herself of late. So she had come alone to the party. Her male and female colleagues at Essi College, where she taught English and Geography, had noticed how she did not reach out to any of them as new comers usually did.

"She thinks she is more beautiful than anybody else," many women gossiped.

"She thinks she is too beautiful to mix with people," others said.

"We'll see what man that beauty will fetch her," a married female teacher added.

Once she had heard of Dede's return and the party, she made up her mind to attend and meet the young man she had heard so much about. She imagined what Dede would look like. Many images of the man milled in her mental landscape. Dede for whose sake she went to the most expensive boutique to buy her pair of shoes worthy of every man's attention. Thinking about Dede had kept her awake to intermittently look at the mirror to be sure that she had the perfect dress for the party. Would he be an *iroko* towering above the forest or a slender palm tree? Or might he be a deer or a warthog? She wondered why she thought of Dede as a plant or an animal. These were what she observed a long time ago when she used to accompany her mother to the farm; plants and animals interested her. Despite these images that crisscrossed her mind, she feared she might be surprised by the real person of Dede.

She soon shifted her curiosity about what type of person Dede would be. A chubby-faced man that is by every measure a gentleman! Perhaps a diminutive man with a vibrant voice! A rugged-looking man that can take on any tasks! Does he walk with a swagger like some of the young men in town who claim to be walking the American style? Will he be bouncing from place to place? Will he speak with the accent of the Americans he had lived with for two years or so? She had become a painter using her mind as a brush to create the features of the person she wanted to meet.

Now at the party, her mind and eyes wandered through the large gathering of young men and women talking, eating, drinking, or dancing. She did not need to be told that Dede was the one whose success was being celebrated. He was very different from the other men around, not just because he had been abroad but perhaps because so. She could not tell why he was so different in a manner that she so easily observed.

Dede stood out in the crowd. It was not because he was the tallest around. Rather, despite his moderate height, he looked distinguished in his demeanour. He wore a dark blue jacket over a light brown sports shirt and brown trousers.

"Here's my man!" she exclaimed silently.

Her heart had spoken before her mouth did. It was a spontaneous response to what she had been expecting after waiting for so long.

For a moment Franka was lost in thought about how to meet this man fresh from another world.

"If I have to do anything to get him as my friend or husband, I will," she told herself.

She wished she possessed the power of a magician or a diviner to either conjure him or cast a spell over him to walk to her. She felt she needed some other power to make things happen the way she wished. She wanted to chat with him and win him over. But she soon realized that she was neither a magician nor a diviner and knew nothing about magic or casting spells. It dawned on her that she had to rely on her human capacity as a woman.

The thought of crossing a river to meet Dede by boat or swimming across to him suddenly came to her. She knew how to swim and in her secondary school days used to swim with several of her schoolmates across the Ethiope River to pick wild mangoes to enjoy. She realized that her days of swimming across a river were over. She was on land at a welcoming party for someone she had not known but looked forward to meeting. She turned every now and then to get a better view of Dede that she upset the glasses of the two men she did not know. "Not yet," she had told the highlife lover when asked for a dance earlier, as she danced tango with Dede in her mental wandering. She quickly regained her composure. She realized that she had to work fast, before the other single ladies around, who would surely be interested in the young man, cornered him into their bosoms.

She decided to do what she had never done before in her life at a party. She instantly made up her mind to go to Dede to ask him for a dance. One step at a time, she calculated. Once they were together, something else would follow, she believed. Immediately some invisible force pulled her from her seat and, without being shy about it, walked gracefully towards Dede. In her specially sewn three-piece yellow traditional attire, and with matching shoes and a handbag, she carried the aura of a beauty queen even though her reign as Miss Delta had ended. Her relative tall height and sparse body had always made her look special.

Dede was chatting with some men and women when she breezed in.

"Excuse me," she said; her voice musically soft and unperturbed by her nervousness.

Dede turned to her. She stood majestically before him. They looked at each other for a moment, her large eyes brilliant. She stepped closer to Dede.

"Can I dance with you?" she asked in an audible whisper.

As if acting on a cue, the D.J. immediately started playing Sonny Okosun's "Fire in Soweto." The D.J. was adept at playing popular records that brought dancers to the floor. The revolutionary voice and percussive rhythm of the song were irresistible.

Dede turned to the small group he was conversing with and bowed gently, a gesture meant to seek permission to leave. He turned back to her.

"Of course, yes," he replied.

They both smiled at each other. His face was smooth and shone with wellbeing, his eyes soft and warm at the same time. His voice attracted her immediately she heard him speak. It was a unique voice, a stream whose current flowed calmly towards the sea.

Dede followed her step after step through the crowd of dancers to the other end of the dimly-lit dance floor. There the spirit of the dance

9

possessed them and they did not only dance to different records but kept to each other for the rest of the party. She sat beside Dede when accolades were poured on him for winning a Federal Government scholarship to study overseas, and for completing his studies in record time and returning rather than staying in the United States.

"You deserve this," she told him.

"Thank you," he replied.

"You must have worked so hard all the time. I understand it is not easy over there," she said.

"I had to do what I went there for and return. A farmer has to return home after the day's task is done," he explained.

"I am proud of you," she said, smiling.

"Thank you," he replied.

Earlier, after their first dance, they had gone through self-introduction and had sat familiarly as if they had come together to the party. As was common of Warri parties, they danced till late into the night and left exhausted.

Three days after the party, to the astonishment of those who knew them, Franka abandoned her teaching and accompanied Dede to Lagos. Gossip flourished. By word of mouth, Warri's telephone without wire, the story passed round, often getting embellished, as more mouths passed along the news of their swift departure from town. Those men that she had rejected said that both she and Dede must have bewitched each other.

"Maybe she wants him to show her the way to the United States," one said.

"Let her follow a pauper if she chooses. When she comes to her proper senses, she will regret not marrying me," a rich chief said of her, when he heard of her disappearance with the newly returned Dede.

"It's because he came from America," some of her colleagues said.

"She must be thinking he is very rich," others said.

The young women who had eyed Dede for a possible suitor or husband said that she had prepared a love potion to win him over to her side. She must have gone to that party prepared and must have added something to Dede's drink or food, once she had pulled him to her side, and that would have made him fall so easily for her, the gossips said.

Before this turn of events, Dede had shunned any serious relationship with women and felt he had not met the one he would share his life with. He had come to this decision after the only woman he really liked while abroad said she was already engaged to somebody else. He had been waiting for a woman he expected to understand and excite him. Someday, he believed, he would meet her and they would know that they had been searching for each other from a teeming crowd. After all, those the gods want to live together will always cross paths. In daylight or on a black-curtained night, it could happen, and he primed himself for the unexpected moment.

Dede had been offered the job of an information officer in the Federal Ministry of Information in Lagos. He wanted to work in a state organ where, he believed, he would make meaningful contribution to his society. The Federal Ministry offered him that opportunity, he thought.

It was Franka's first visit to Lagos and she instantly fell in love with the big city. All she would need as a happy woman would be available there, she suddenly realized. Clothes, jewellery, cars, and whatever luxuries a woman needed were there to purchase. There was glamour, if she wanted it. No wonder her schoolmates at St. Ita's Girls Grammar School, Sapele, used to be so excited at narrating their vacation experiences in Lagos. The city that in those days appeared unreachable was now her new home. Every day she spent in Lagos made her wish not to leave there for anywhere else. Lagos cast a spell on her and she succumbed to the city's charm.

Neither she nor he was in doubt that they were going to share their lives together. Lagos kept them busy. He went to work very early to avoid the notorious traffic jam and returned late, as she spent time finding her way to interview for a teaching position. Still, they found time to go back to Delta State for their traditional wedding and then come back to Lagos for a court marriage. She failed to persuade him for a wedding in the Catholic Church that he described as an imperial power.

2

Franka was only ten years old when her father died from snakebite in the farm. It was a hot and humid afternoon in the dry season, when, according to elders, snakes became restless and roamed the bush to relieve themselves of the choking poison in them. She would, for many years, carry the mental picture of her father sweating profusely, groaning, and hopping on one leg from the farm; his face contorted by pain. He muttered "Cobra!" with shaky lips. Pressed on, he barely said out that as his machete descended on some weeds a cobra rose from their midst to strike him. The snake was too fast for his machete. It had a direct hit on his right leg that within minutes started to swell and give excruciating pain. Every passing moment made the pain worse and by the time he got home it was smothering his breath.

The villagers' effort to catch or kill the snake in order to extract its poison to treat him with it failed not only because they could not find it, but they wasted valuable time that could have saved his life. A cobra knows its way in the forest as humans know theirs in town. Nobody thought of rushing him to a hospital ten miles away in Sapele because they were all scared off by the terrible cost of treatment. He stretched on a mat surrounded by older men talking loudly but not making sense to Franka watching from the doorside. She cried because her mother was crying and she soon realized that her father was gone.

By the time of his death, Udi had passed his prime and was already on the decline. So, the farmer that used to harvest huge yams that filled several barns could only reap enough to make a little money and feed the four mouths in the family. His loss was still devastating to his wife and children whose helper had been snatched away by fate. Franka's uncles on both sides were themselves not doing well and so could not support her mother to take care of her and her only brother. They tapped their ageing rubber trees and made too little money from the exhausting work to live on and still spend on others. Since there was nobody in the extended family that did well then, Franka, her mother, and brother were left alone to fend for themselves.

Though young, Franka knew how hard things were for them at the time. Her only sibling and brother, three years her junior, died mysteriously within a year of losing her father. In hindsight, her brother might have been saved with a small amount. There was no money to take him to the hospital and he must have died of typhoid or malaria fever, she now believed. Only forty naira might have saved him, but such was the degree of their hardship that her mother could not raise that amount and had to look on helplessly as her son's condition deteriorated until he died in the house. That was another sad picture frozen in her mind.

Her mother realized that she had to work tirelessly to save herself and her surviving child from starving. She farmed cassava to make *garri* for their consumption and for sale to make some money to buy a few necessities. It was a big struggle for her to go to a secondary school, which she cried all the time she must attend. She saw young girls of about her age already in secondary schools and during vacation proudly introducing themselves and the schools they were attending. *One day, I am going to stand up and say I am Franka Udi, a student of St. Mary Magdalene Grammar School or whatever school I will attend. I will wear my neat uniform so that everybody will know that I am a very good student. I want to carry my head high. I will do well at school to make my mother proud of me. I will be very happy if she is proud of me.* She reflected much on her future in school.

"You know I won't be able to pay your school fees and buy your uniform and books," her mother had told her.

"You can do it. I will help you," she had responded.

"How?" the mother had asked, unsure of what she was asking, her ability to pay or how she, so young, would help to pay for her own school fees.

A mother intuitively feels her daughter's passion for something. She knew that Franka's desire to go to a secondary school came from deep inside her and she agreed to do her best to assist her. She had to put a load on the daughter's head that she could carry without being crushed under it. She had already heard her neighbours' snipes at her as the woman who did not rest but worked day and night. Let them gossip about her as they wished, she told herself; she had no help as other women had with their husbands or relatives. She saw herself as the tailless cow whose tormenting flies had to be driven away for her by God.

The Almighty alone had to be her support in raising her daughter, she believed. She felt fortunate that there was available land to farm and so determined to help her daughter at school. That meant planting or harvesting cassava during the day and frying *garri* till late in the night.

Franka entered St. Ita's Girls' Grammar School, Sapele, not sure that she would complete her secondary schooling because of lack of adequate money to pay school fees and meet other needs. On her outing day, the first Saturday of the month, she went to help her mother to work in the cassava farm or prepare *garri*. Frying *garri* meant sitting by blazing fire outside for hours usually in the late afternoon or evening, though Franka had to help when she could in the late morning and afternoon.

"Don't be blinded by the smoke and heat. You need good eyes to read your books," her mother would warn.

"I won't be blind. You can't do everything yourself," she would respond.

She constantly wiped her face dripping with sweat; her whole body wet. Her clothes soaked in perspiration clung to her.

She hurriedly took a bath, packed for snacks some of the regular *garri* and *kpokpo garri* she had helped to prepare in a black polythene bag, and rushed back to school. Nobody knew what she had gone out to do. She used the same dresses all year round. Fortunately, at school they wore two types of uniform, the white one for classes and the khaki one in the hostel. She kept her dresses neat and nobody really knew the extent of her need.

During vacations, in addition to assisting her mother in the farm, she fried and sold *akara* to make money towards her next school fees. In the early morning, she waited for buyers and by late morning, not wanting to throw the remaining ones away and lose money, she balanced a platter of *akara* on her head and hawked them from street to street. Some older men and women pitied her and bought whatever was left for her to return home. When her mother saw her sweating and working so hard as if her survival depended on farming and frying *garri* and *akara* at that tender age, she felt like crying.

"Maybe if your father were alive, you wouldn't be working this hard. Some of your age-mates are already getting married. Don't you think you should save yourself the sweat and dirt of farming by marrying?"

"Do married women not farm?" she asked her mother.

"Yes, they do but not your type," she told her.

"No, Mama, I don't want to marry yet. I want to remain in school," she would reply.

14

Her mother kept mum, holding back tears at seeing her only child not enjoy her years as a youth. Franka did not attend many social gatherings that her fellow secondary schoolmates frequented. She often gave the excuse that she was not feeling fine, but went on those evenings and early nights to help her mother fry *garri*. She heard the booming music of her partying mates as she toiled, but that did not distract her. She knew her fate depended on how much *garri* her mother sold in the market.

She imagined what her mother was feeling and tried to ease her agony for her.

"When I bathe, the sweat and dirt disappear. Am I not more beautiful than those who don't work?" she asked her.

"You are more beautiful than your age-mates, my daughter. God made you well," her mother told her with a nod and a warm smile.

She knew that her daughter's beauty was not common. She felt happy for her.

"Don't worry about me. I'll finish my school," she affirmed.

"Okay-o," the mother would tell her in a wavering tone.

She wanted her daughter to marry so as to be attached to somebody who would take care of her, but she would not deliberately abort her strong desire for school. One of Franka's early suitors that she turned down at that time, because she was not ready for marriage, would become a rich chief after winning many government contracts because he wrote in *The Daily News* that General Ogiso should be given a chance to develop the country. At a time when the general was under siege from all directions, this was a positive respite for him; hence the sympathetic writer's reward. That husband she missed had many estates in Sapele. Franka hoped what she missed because of education she would more than gain also through education someday.

After the long vacation, she listened to her schoolmates talk about the exotic places they had visited. Some had gone to Lagos, others to Ibadan and Kaduna. A few students, daughters of very rich parents, told their fairytales of flying to London where they had experienced paradise.

"Buckingham Palace was a great spectacle. The change of guards was so colourful. The Queen was driven out of the palace in a horse-drawn coach when I was there," Ufuoma said.

"Hyde Park was my favourite spot," Margaret said.

Franka did not open her mouth. She knew her schoolmates would not be impressed by her working in the farm or selling *akara*. If she told them that she went to comb for snails to sell, they would laugh hilariously at her for exposing herself to thorns, cockleburs, and snakes in the forest. She wanted to stay in school by all means, if that meant she had to go fishing in the nearby creeks with older women to catch fish for sale.

Whenever she saw women teachers, she saw something that she wanted to become. They were neat and they dressed well. They had acquired so much knowledge from their readings. Above all, men and women respected female teachers. She made up her mind that she would one day become a teacher. With that in mind, nothing would move her away from school to marry as her mother was persuading her to do. She was able to complete her secondary school. She made very good grades in all her seven subjects.

Her hunger for higher education took her to the College of Education, Abraka, where she was fortunate to win a State-wide beauty contest in her first semester. That provided her enough money, since winning the contest included a big cash award. She appeared on local television. Newspapers and magazines interviewed her. The public exposure brought many more suitors. Most of these suitors were divorcees and widowers, fairly old people who wanted her so they could boast of having a beautiful young wife. She wanted her future husband to be older than her, but she would not be a replacement at the hands of a husband far older than her. Other men wanted her but just to sleep with. She knew that was not her life.

To save herself from men, who swore that they loved her despite the lust bristling in their eyes, she made up her mind from that time to marry when the opportunity came as soon as she graduated. She could not rely on boyfriends. She wanted a man she could call her husband. She wanted to live a decent life. She wanted a family of her own.

The line of suitors became interminable after her graduation. She was a trophy waiting to be snatched by one of them. She would be the rare feather to adorn their hats. With her they would be unparalleled chiefs, those men believed. However, she wanted none of these suitors. Much as she wanted to marry, she wanted somebody she really loved, somebody she would live the rest of her life with. She wanted whomever she married to always stir excitement in her. These suitors were all too tame and mundane for her.

3

Dede's salary in the Federal Ministry of Information was a pittance. His starting salary was two scales above what first degree graduates in the civil service earned. Promotion to senior information officer or even chief information officer did little to raise the annual salary to a substantial amount. Nobody entered the civil service to become rich, the saying went. It was a tortoise race that made little impression as far as distance was concerned, unless the tortoise used its cunning to ride on a fast animal's back. Dede was not going to take the shortcut to material gain.

With an M.A. in public communication and specialization in print media, he, to Franka, was wasting his time in the civil service that he wanted to change. To her, he was squandering his time that could better be utilized in a different way. She believed life was a race and choosing the tortoise pace instead of springing was unacceptable. He had more than the legs of a dog; he could be a cheetah if he harnessed his resources which were many and superior, as far as she knew.

Dede complained about everything. People did not work hard. They spent their time reading newspapers, telephoning, and gossiping when they should be working. There was over-employment and yet a heavy backlog of work at all times. The pending file of every senior officer was a mountain of confusion. Many graduate employees did not use the skills they had acquired in the university because they were only carrying files from one desk to another. They wasted too much paper. His complaints were endless. Was it not called civil service or bureaucracy because things hardly changed? she asked him.

He ignored her plea to apply to Shell Company for a public relations job, since he had the right qualification. In those days, there could have been no difficulty getting such a job. In fact, such positions were advertised in the papers. But he kept to his dream of changing the attitude of civil servants from a moribund to a dynamic state in which things worked efficiently. It was as if he wanted to take over the work of his superior officers and do their work for them—sign papers as soon as they arrived on the desk; be prudent with government materials and funds; use time judiciously; and a litany of what made efficient work.

His complaints and wishes continued to increase and he began to be seen as an obstacle to the civil service work culture. He was in the office on time, often waiting for a long time for the doors to be opened. He did not allow the doors of his office to be shut until it was actual closing time. He went on this way until a secondary school graduate, who had risen to a senior administrative officer position, fired him for insubordination. He would not do the work of three other information officers who regularly did not show up for work but collected their salaries at the end of every month. No senior officer read his long letters complaining about the ineptitude of the officer who dismissed him.

He was lucky that a new newspaper started recruiting qualified people for its editorial positions. That was how he entered *The African Patriot*. He suddenly had a new platform to try to change things nationwide. He became more vociferous and cared not for his safety, as if his life was only his and not shared by his wife and later by his kids also. Secret service men had visited the house when he was not in several times, as if they deliberately chose the time to come in. They had manhandled her and she was lucky that they did not rape her on any of the occasions, but she was very scared. She had reported to Dede the incidents, but he preached to her that they had to make sacrifices for the sake of the general good of the country. She could not understand the general good in their being harassed and living under the constant threat of arrest or even death. One day she would be raped and he would still dismiss it as part of the sacrifice for the general good of the country, she thought.

And it really happened. One day she was abducted by a group of soldiers looking for Dede. It appeared they had gone to his office and did not find him there. They pushed her into their van and took her away. There she struggled unsuccessfully from being violated by two of the abductors, after which she was driven back and left in the house. She could not reveal this to Dede, but she expected him to know from her depressed mood. Several times she wanted to say it but she was afraid of his reaction. Would he not throw himself into the lion's den? He was no Daniel and bore no charmed life to survive, she knew. The secret service agents could be looking for an opportunity to kill him, and his explosion if she had told him that she was raped would be the beginning of the end. Maybe a woman does not have to reveal everything to her husband. A few things might be better kept secret for their own good, she reflected. She gave up telling him about her being raped but lived with the double guilt of being violated and not informing her husband about it. He was so preoccupied with his ambition to remain a human rights hero that he did not notice her agony.

While he was unaware of her agony, he talked all the time about Mrs. Eunice Fatumbi, whom he described as a brilliant schoolteacher. Franka became suspicious since he did not stop talking about how great and intelligent this woman was. One day when she stopped by his office, she learnt that he had gone to Akowe High School where Mrs. Fatumbi taught and she could see why he praised her all the time. The way the office attendant looked at her made her feel there was something going on between Dede and the woman. She must be coming to see him too in the office, she believed.

When Dede came home very late that evening, Franka told him she had been to his office in the early afternoon. She wanted him to say where he went to at the time so as to clear himself on his relationship with Mrs. Fatumbi. She stared at him to observe his body language even as he spoke to her.

"I was out investigating some scams," he told her.

"What scams?" she asked.

"You know corruption is endemic to this country and it rears its ugly head here and there," he explained.

"I thought you drove to Akowe High School at the time," she said.

She waited for what he would say. Accept or deny? She held her breath for what would come out of his mouth.

"Who told you that?" he asked.

"Nobody, I just guessed so."

"Have you been trailing me? I was out doing my job," he said.

She felt no need to pursue this argument. Dede would not admit to visiting Mrs. Fatumbi, she believed.

She would hear from gossip later that the woman's husband did not really care about what she did. Then she met Mrs. Fatumbi and hated her instantly. She hated her confidence and liberal manners, hated her pretty looks, and hated especially her air of familiarity with Dede. What was going on between these two people? she asked herself.

But worse still, their financial situation did not improve with the coming of the two children and he would not seek a job in a company. He had a new dream to rattle the Leopard and bring down a military

19

government with his pen. He wanted to wrestle with the Python of Deep Waters and win. He wanted to knock down the Elephant that had never fallen. He wanted to de-fang the Cobra with his pen.

"Won't you tone down your writing?" she would ask.

"Are you asking me to abandon my duty to society?" he would ask back.

"The job is not worth the risk. You may be known, but na fame we go chop?" she queried in a sarcastic tone.

His frequent absence from home on assignments did not help matters either. He left for distant states for days to get to the bottom of a story. He volunteered too often to carry out the paper's investigative work as if he was the only one who could do such an assignment.

His columns were popular. But popularity would not feed them, nor would it buy them a new car. Living comfortably was a basic right of the family, she told him. Whenever she suggested that he should get another job to make more money, he asked her to share his poverty with him or leave it to him alone. He could barely maintain the used Datsun car he bought several years back. It broke down almost every week and it had to be jacked up and left alone till he got enough money to have it repaired and put back on the road. They lived in a two-bedroom flat, which became too small once children started arriving, but they had to keep on managing.

He kept on insisting that money was not important to happiness. She did not buy his argument. To her, it was not a matter of money as such; it was a matter of comfort. She wanted to live comfortably and that meant eating well, dressing beautifully, and having a car of her own, if possible. These basic needs were within their reach, she felt, if he changed his job. She had to forfeit the mudfish she liked to eat because it was too expensive. She also liked to eat *bush* meat, which, because expensive, she had to pass for common beef. Chicken was reserved for special occasions. She went to the food market and suffered the humiliation of being insulted for haggling too long by the fish sellers, who knew other women would pay whatever price they asked for. She felt all of them in the family deserved to eat what they desired. How long does one live to spend so many years in avoidable penury? she asked. They had continued to manage one thing after the other, and lack of adequate money to spend had given a frugal pattern to their lives.

She wanted a different lifestyle that would make her feel good about herself and that involved comfort that money would provide. He had so many chances to get a job that would bring in more money, as she saw it, but was either too idealistic or too egotistical to see the other side of things. Every man should provide adequately for his family if it was within his means, she thought. She could not have suffered all her childhood and teenage years and still continue to suffer in her marriage life. She knew already what suffering meant and she wanted to keep away from it as far as she could.

The tension in the reciprocal relationship between happiness and money remained unresolved. Soon Dede returned from work, ate, and went straight to bed. Franka now discovered that he snored in an irritating manner that kept her awake till late in the night. She now hated his unkempt beard, finger and toe nails. They slept at opposite ends of their bed without any effort to cross over to the other. Dede woke early and did not like Franka's makeup as he saw her sleeping. Dede did not like the way she coughed, as if choked, while asleep. By the time both of them were up and doing their toiletries, the other's spitting or gurgling enervated the other. Also Franka was disturbed by Dede's loud talking as if she were not in the same room.

Once it became loveless, their marriage was doomed. They drifted apart and looked for excuses to terminate the marriage that neither of them wanted to continue.

Despite the problems, it was a miracle that they had gone on to have two children and the marriage had lasted seven years.

"May God bless you in your endeavours," she told him, as she left their home for the last time. She could no longer bear to stay in what she considered a prison.

"May God bless you too," Dede replied, also feeling relieved from what had become a perennial bad situation.

4

As the date of the court hearing for the divorce drew close, the two, as if planning for a moral battle, thought of inventing vices to tarnish the other. Their lawyers had coached them respectively on what to say; they coached from the same book on divorce.

"Be consistent, never blink—say whatever you say loud and clear and in a confident manner. Enunciate your words. The magistrate was never in your bedroom. Present your case in a credible way and you will win. Winning is the bottom line."

Dede knew that in their culture, women had to be accused of witchcraft and adultery to seal their doom both in the law court and in the court of public opinion. Those labels were like a poison-charm placed on a fruiting tree; they would drive men away from her. She would be worse than a scarecrow to men who remained superstitious despite their embrace of Christianity. He knew that ignorance fostered the belief in witchcraft, but that did not stop him from calling his enemy a witch. Franka had changed from a loved one, a darling, to an enemy.

On her side, she liked the court of law. She felt fortunate that she was educated and not just an illiterate woman who might not know her rights. A secondary school education and the three years at the College of Education, Abraka, had exposed her to the ways of the world. Once married in the court, a man could not keep another woman as a girlfriend or a concubine. That would mean cheating and adultery, serious infractions of the marriage act. The woman was not just helpless in marriage, but could seek redress if offended. That was the best thing the British left, a strong rope to restrain the men from their goatish habits, she thought. Thanks to the British, she could seek redress, she assured herself. She could use the court to cut Dede down to his proper size.

At first she had been worried about seeking a divorce. She had not married hoping to one day divorce her husband. She had always wanted a stable family life. But now she wanted a divorce because she could not live in poverty and fear all her life. However much she tried to explain to him, Dede would not understand. She had suffered silently and he did not bother about her agony, which marriage to him had caused her. Nor would she share her husband with someone else. She would accuse him of sleeping around, never coming to her bed. He used his journalist's career as an excuse to go out as he wished. After all, she knew one case that he would always deny and say was ordinary friendship but she suspected was a much deeper relationship.

She would say that he beat her when he came back drunk early in the morning from his trysts with his many girlfriends. She would say that she had been beaten even when she was pregnant. She would use the burn marks she had sustained accidentally when a child as evidence of his physical abuse of her. They had always remained covered, but she would not mind to bare her right shoulder for the court to see proof of Dede's cruelty. She would say that he had pushed her into the gas cooker and she got burned. She knew magistrates would convict a man for neglecting and abusing his wife. All she wanted was justifiable evidence to ask for a divorce. She wanted the blame to be placed on the man and not on herself.

"Dede is the cruellest man on earth," her lady attorney told her to repeat.

"Stress it as much as you can and explode in tears. Every judge is human and where words fail to move, tears can. Don't fail to cry out. Be hysterical. Who would allow his sister or daughter to be wife to a cruel man? Your Lordship, none!"

They felt elated in a self-congratulatory manner, slapping each other's right palm. They had woven a perfect net to catch Dede and there was no way they imagined that he would slip out of it. They would continue squeezing his balls till he begged for forgiveness and let her go her own way.

They engaged each other like primitive mastodons fighting for survival. Neither one would relent in the pursuit of atrocious inventions until the other was defeated and humiliated. The magistrate granted them the divorce they sought.

Savage as the divorce case was, the battle for custody over the children was much uglier than both of them could have imagined. The matter had gone too far. Dede wanted to keep the two children. He

23

couldn't bring himself to believe that a divorced woman could take proper care of children. If she dated or married another man, how was she going to properly take care of the children? He felt she might even hide the children so that she would be seen as single.

He totally ignored the reasons why he, a journalist, a working man, and soon to be unattached as well, might not be a good single parent either. He did not ask himself who was going to take care of the children when he was out pursuing news.

"If you think you're going to live on my money, you are wrong, dead wrong. Over my dead body will any court order me to pay you anything monthly. There will be neither alimony nor child support allowance. I would rather live a bankrupt man so that no kobo will leave my account to one woman so she can spend it on her lovers. No way!" he shouted, as if he was answering some objectionable question. Franka knew very well that he had no money to pay out to her. This fact soon dawned on him as well.

He felt like someone pushed into a pit and scrambling to get out. In the process, he almost buried himself alive. He hated himself for the inventions he had composed to make a pariah of Franka, but he felt that in war one had to use the meanest weapons and tactics to ensure victory. There were experiences, he realized, which only reduced you to the lowest point of the bottom. Divorce and child custody battles were such experiences.

Franka also felt that once she had fallen in the mud that she had to not only roll in it but drag her adversary as deep into it as she possibly could. She had been called the worst of names, witch and adulteress. She had lost her good reputation and there was nothing more left for her to lose. She had wanted a good family life, but that hope was now shattered. Who would believe her that she was a simple village girl who scratched a living with her mother and worked hard to go to school? Who would believe that she did not like divorce but a happy married life? Men she would meet would believe what had been said about her because people believed that a man knew his wife best and vice versa. Now she had to roll in this filth with Dede. That had meant a shameless series of actions.

Now she realized she could not extricate herself from the net of malice she had woven. It had been thrown over herself as well as Dede. Her former honey, Dede, had become an enemy that she had to crush. Was she not the charming Franka that so many suitors were after until she gave her nod to him without playing hard to get? She had tried to counter his accusations with her own inventions.

"If you feel you can destroy me and remain whole, you must be joking. Either you get crushed alone or the two of us are eliminated together. I don't mind that. Either I win or we both lose. You have to regret this all of your life so that in your next life, you will not take any woman for granted. As you have stripped me naked, so too will I expose you to the world and parade you through the streets. I will paint you into a scarecrow." She now saw the truth of the traditional saying that one who talks to oneself surely has a problem. She had a problem on her hands.

Her mother and friends had supported her leaving Dede whom she accused of calling her a witch and an adulteress. She swore to them that she was neither. She could not tell her mother and friends that she had been raped by soldiers because of him; she could not bring herself to say it to them too. She could not tell the world about her past suffering and her aim in life to live well. Nor would she be telling her mother and friends about the battles she consistently waged with Dede for money to buy things. And she could not tell her friends and mother about her strong suspicion that he was having an affair with another woman he must have known a long time back when in America.

Where the mastodons fought, the grass was bound to suffer. Five-year old Uvie and eighteen-month old Kena became the grass that bore the brunt of the savage fight that their parents etched deeper with inattention to them, as they thought only of themselves. Kena had started to walk in the house but was always attached to her mother, who was weaning her out of breast milk into solid foods. She was too small to know what was happening.

Uvie intuitively knew the change in the house but could not fully understand why Daddy and Mommy were now like strangers to him and his small sister. At kindergarten school, when asked about his parents, he said they were fine. That was what everybody said. But while other mothers and fathers came in one car to drop or collect every other kid, only his father or mother came for him. Even that was for some time because, later, it was just his father alone. From the shouts, accusations, and later the absence of Mom, who took Kena along, he had the feeling that something was wrong between his parents.

"Where is Mommy?" he often asked his dad.

"She travelled," the father told his young son.

"When is she coming back?" Uvie asked.

"I don't know."

The child's face told his confusion about his mother's long travel without returning home.

The two children had not been taken to court during the divorce hearing. But for the custody case, they were the chief exhibits to be displayed and used to help each parent's case. The social worker argued that Kena was just too young to leave her mother. Besides, there was no way a male journalist could care for a baby girl alone, the social worker declared.

Dede's mother, who had taken Kena for two weeks, was in court. She had gone to Franka when she was at her friend Ebi's house to take her granddaughter and she had surrendered her daughter then to relieve both Ebi and her of so much pressure. Now there was a big uproar as Dede's mother refused to give up her granddaughter to Franka, whom she called an untrustworthy woman. She had only heard her son's narrative of events that he had described as unbearable for any husband. The grandmother held Kena by the arms and her mother held the little girl's legs in a tug-of-war to keep the child.

"It's my child!" Franka shouted.

"It's my son's child!" Dede's mother shouted back.

The police intervened and gave the child to Franka.

Dede had custody of Uvie. He had the means to take care of him, the social worker argued. In the end, neither father nor mother had any voice in the outcome of the custody battle. The social worker had assigned each child, basing her judgment on what she had deemed best for each child, irrespective of the parents' separate claims, and the court upheld her recommendations despite Dede and Franka's objections.

Franka and Dede were known in many social circles in Lagos, and *The Lagos Weekend* exploited their recognition for its maximum benefit. A former beauty queen and an overseas-trained activist journalist were not common people. The reportage was certainly a deliberate overkill, but that was what *The Lagos Weekend* enjoyed doing.

Their story covered the front page and spilled over into the third page. The writers' abiding philosophy was that whatever people enjoyed should be prolonged for as long as possible.

NATIONAL PAPER EDITOR IN DIVORCE PALAVER

A respected editor of a national paper, an award-winning essayist, a nationally and internationally known human rights activist, has been thrown into a bitter divorce battle with his wife of seven years. They have accused each other of attempting to use poison or hired assassins to eliminate the other. Both have fled their matrimonial home for safety as each mobilizes forces to counteract the other. The whereabouts of their children are unknown. From the grapevine we have learnt that each has taken a lover for an attorney in their expected battle of the giants...

Another caption read: MY HUSBAND CANNOT PERFORM—DISSATISFIED EDITOR'S WIFE. "A former local beauty queen married for seven years splits with her husband over boring sex and other secret reasons," the paper began. "Both partners have sought pleasure outside their home until the woman hired a detective who caught the man with another woman in a hotel. That other woman was the wife's best friend that used to come and visit them in their marital home," it continued.

The Lagos Weekend's reporters vied to have their own caption blaze the front page. It was a fierce competition to write the story that would be the talk of the town and perhaps the whole nation the entire weekend. At the end of the year, awards for the most captivating stories were handed out and whoever won the coveted story of the year not only took away a cash prize but also a trophy.

Dede, who had always enjoyed the usually outrageous cover stories of *The Lagos Weekend* and did not miss reading the juicy and often salacious paper on Friday morning, now knew what it felt like being the subject of a publicized scandal. He realized too the wisdom in the saying, "Another man head na coconut!" Others were enjoying the scandal at his expense.

5

Within a few weeks after the split-even verdict of the child custody case, it dawned on Franka what it meant to be a single working mother. It was true that Dede was a busy man, but he had helped in sharing some of the chores and errands. Now she had to do everything herself and she had no car. At times she became paralyzed by confusion. She spent time thinking about how to resolve simple things she should do. She discovered that the divorce had complicated her life. *God, help me cope with my daily tasks,* she prayed silently. *I need the energy of three people to do my work if I am not going to break down. I need a trinity of powers to be saved from this hell.* When in difficulty, and she needed a quick solution, she turned to her Catholic faith for succour. She soon realized, as her problem intensified, that praying was not enough to get out of the hell into which she had fallen.

She had rented a one-bedroom flat even before the divorce was finalized. Earlier she had stayed at her friend Ebi's for three weeks, but that was when she was looking for a flat to rent for herself. Her belongings cluttered the place and she knew she was bothering her friend. Two women waiting for each other to use the bathroom or dressing mirror first, to her, was not a good way of living. Nor was it fair to either of them deciding what food to cook that both would like. She liked *banga* soup, Ebi preferred *egusi* soup. She ate *eba* while her friend took semolina. Their choices of meat and fish to eat were also different and one had to give in to the other's favourite. Neither of the two was living a full life as long as they shared one flat. Ebi told her that she could live with her for as long as it would take for her to get a new accommodation, but she felt the earlier she was independent the better for her future life.

She moved to her own place soon after she almost set Ebi's home on fire. She had taken from her matrimonial home many copies of *The Lagos Weekend*. She used to like reading the paper but she had become so disgusted with the reporting of her cases with Dede that she made a pile of the past issues in the courtyard, doused them with kerosene, and set them on fire. If she were not fast enough, the wind would have blown the fire to consume the flat and the entire building. For months afterwards, she often dreamt of a wild blaze in which she and Dede were trapped. Her nights tortured her with fire just as her days did.

Alone, she could not manage her daughter and her teaching job at Command Secondary School, Ojo. She needed help. Prayers could not deliver her the trinity of powers to work the miracle she desperately needed to keep her sanity. She could not afford to pay for a maid to help her take care of Kena. Rent, taxi to work, and food consumed all she earned. In addition, she had heard bad stories about maids in Lagos and she did not want to trust her daughter with any of them. She also thought of bringing a young relative from home but there was none in her family to bring. There was the problem of the one-bedroom to share with whomever she brought. There was no easy option, she soon realized. She hurriedly took the baby girl to her mother at Arhagba in Delta State. Her mother was happy to have her granddaughter live with her.

The big city was where the action was, she told herself. Once you have lived in Lagos, no other place in the country would be good enough; hence you got stuck to it. *Am I not a Lagosian?* she asked herself. She responded affirmatively to her own question. She would live her life and enjoy it in Lagos. This city was already an inseparable part of her life that she had to cope with, no matter what happened.

But considerations of company or friends apart, she wanted to do something extra to make money. Only Lagos offered her the opportunity to realize that. If one really worked hard and put one's mind and heart into any business in Lagos, one could make plenty of money. Let Dede squander his potentials; she was ready to exploit hers for maximum gain. She had not made up her mind about what else she could do to supplement her teaching salary, but the possibilities were plentiful ahead. She could sell women's dresses, underwear, perfumes, watches, bags, and shoes. With most of her colleagues the wives of rich army officers, that would not be a bad business to start with, since they had more than enough money to spend to look fine.

She was determined to be strong. Only the strong succeed; the weak fail, she told herself. She had to succeed to prove to Dede that a woman's life does not end with divorce, but that, in fact, the real fun begins after it. She knew she had to take the road to prosperity and follow it doggedly. Dede had been too dumb to listen to her. She hated poverty. Her childhood days knew harsh poverty and it was something that she would flee from at all costs. Was everybody's prayer not for prosperity? She needed to prosper and live a good life. She might meet a man that she loved and who also loved her and they could marry and settle down. She still believed in the settled life that marriage brought about. She realized that some marriages did not work, but that did not mean that marriage was bad. She wanted a good family life.

6

Dede had always hated General Ogiso and for good reasons. During what would be the last months of the Shehu Administration, Dede was nominated for the National Merit Award. He did not know who nominated him but he was one of the five shortlisted candidates for the prestigious award that was not given to anyone that year because one morning the people woke to the brazen sound of martial music. In the face of the cancellation of normal radio and television programs was the announcement of an army takeover of government. That was six and a half years ago.

General Ogiso came into office with a seductive smile; he glittered with brass medals. He dressed smartly in his deep green uniform and cut the image of a confident general. In his first broadcast to the nation, he promised to make life comfortable for everyone. He would lead the people from suffering to salvation; he would clear the whole country of thorns, he would lead his fellow citizens to the rainbow's end and seize the diamond from the mouth of the cobra guarding it. The country would be rich, everybody would be rich, and they would have a foretaste of heaven before they died.

Security, the self-proclaimed president emphasized from the beginning, was the key to the survival of his regime. He wanted to be on guard at every moment because every soldier in the country dreamed of seizing power and he would not be a victim of a counter-coup. He had to be firm and so had his eyes and ears everywhere imaginable to catch any mischievous person or group plotting against him. He would pay as many people as possible to spy for him and also pay others to spy on the spies. One of the rules of his government was not to trust anybody except himself. Everybody else was his potential enemy. The only loyalty he would reluctantly trust would be that of his paid agents. As for loyalty out of love, he did not believe it existed in the country.

In General Ogiso's rule some customs thought to be long gone resurfaced. He offered human sacrifices to gods and spirits to ward off death. The corridors of power filled with flies and putrid stench assaulted the polity. Nobody would mind if the chief executive wiped out all the goats, rams, and cows that oftentimes constituted a nuisance to drivers and pedestrians as offerings to the spirits he wanted to protect him. He would be helping to keep Lagos clean in his own way by ridding the streets of animal shit. But instead of beasts, he chose human beings. The gods of fear must be appeased before the president went to bed so as to have sweet dreams of being not only the richest man in the world but also the longest surviving president in Africa, which held that record for the world. His diviners needed human skulls in order to pray for no wizard or witch in the land to interfere with his vital organs while asleep.

The president's men also swept the expected route of His Excellency several hours before he passed. Every road that he passed on land, in the air, and on water had to be closed for three hours to every other traveller until he had passed. They were working on the technology for him to travel underground, but that would take many years or even decades to achieve.

Those who grew long beards had to be detained and tortured as terrorists; hence Dede Daro and his kind with cropped beards were seen as national irritants taunting the rage of the president. Many mullahs grumbled, but invoking their religion's dictates mattered not to the president and they complied. Respect and fear had to go together in the people's relationship with their leader, the president believed. The general carried either a crocodile-inscribed swagger-stick or a fly-whisk, imbued with magical power, to ward off evil.

Nobody was allowed to build more than a one-story house near the president's residence, since it was assumed that from a higher height one could see the inside of the mansion and this would make His Excellency vulnerable to snipers. Sharpshooters took up defensive and offensive positions on the hill site of the presidential mansion. They looked down on the rest of the city dwellers and stopped any disconcerting move before it reached a dangerous stage.

President Ogiso took over some people's wives to increase his harem; others he raped and sent back to their husbands. Nobody told the sorrow of many of his ministers whose wives he asked to visit him and they usually did in order to save their husbands from unimagined danger. The general took the praise-names of Leopard and Cock. The leopard was the general of the forest. The cock ushered in dawn. He also called himself *Agbraran*! Lightning burns anything on its path. Still he called on his diviners for every phenomenon that threatened his assumed power to control everything. They always divined good tidings for him even in the face of a raging storm.

Dede wrote a poem which he kept to himself because the Leopard's anger could only be appeased with blood. He would not give his blood in that cheap way.

The Accusation

King of Skyland,
I accuse you
of inflicting a desert on our lives;
it has swamped us to the neck
in doomsday dunes.
I accuse you
of pillaging wombs for foetuses
to perform diabolic rituals,
of breaking balls of celibates
to squeeze out semen
for a drink to outlive the sun,
of fuelling a dynastic bonfire
with bones of skinned prophets.
I accuse you
of wiping out smiles from faces
and smiting them with warts,
of inaugurating this vast prison
in which we hang heels up.
I accuse you
of decreeing the foothold of our nativity
into a firing range
where crowds are cross-fired
to serve the monster god of government.
I accuse you
of tearing us from the eagle's loft,
of crippling our galloping horse,
of binding us hands and feet
and throwing the sack into a sea of sharks.
King of Skyland,
I accuse you.

7

Now that the divorce was complete and the child custody battle over, Dede wanted to put the unpleasant experiences behind him and forge ahead. He would now concentrate on his journalism, do his job at *The African Patriot*, and freelance for any local or international papers that sought his work. The ripples of his last article had not yet subsided, and many believed they never would as long as President Ogiso ruled the land. The general possessed the unforgiving memory of the cobra whose venom remains vaulted in its small brain until it decides to attack.

The piece titled "The African Cannibal Clique" in *Time Magazine* was signed by David Rupert. Every distinguished journalist in the nation knew who David Rupert was from the subject, style, and tone of the writing. In fact, it was the editors of the American international newsmagazine that had asked Dede to use a pseudonym, because, so often in the past ten years, many of their brilliant African correspondents had disappeared after writing such an investigative report.

There was barely any serious digging deep in Africa without uncovering dirt that embarrassed the political leaders. Where was Kimuyu Nananga of Nairobi now? Dead! What happened to Chimombo Zewa of Zomba? Dead! What also happened to Masinga Ndolo of Kinshasa? Dead! The litany of dead journalists went on and on. These African writers had disappeared, evaporated, been swallowed by crocodiles or fatally stung by chameleons. Only in Africa do writers and journalists who criticize the political leaders "evaporate" like vapour from the face of the earth. Only in Africa do crocodiles come to land to swallow adults who raised their voices against tyranny. Also only in Africa do chameleons exercise fatal stings against irritants of corrupt governments.

Dede was grateful for the foresight of *Time*'s editorial board for shielding him from the leopard that would not have hesitated to either pounce on him or send his cubs against him. Either experience would have been extremely dangerous and resulted in his dying or getting maimed permanently. Franka had advised him to be careful, but in these circumstances how careful could he be, if he wanted to live and do his job well? Surely, the smart Americans saved his blood from being used to appease the spirits that daily haunted the president.

He had written the article while already estranged from Franka, but before the divorce and custody court appearances. He saw plenty of evidence to show that African military leaders learned from each other how to devastate their own countries. They had an informal association of living and dead military dictators that met to invoke the spirit of their cannibal progenitor. Idi Amin, Bokasa (the self-proclaimed butcher of Bangui), Mobutu, Nguema, and Ogiso were all cannibals, plundering their nations as no plague in history ever did. He was not surprised that they all proclaimed themselves generals or marshals, the highest military positions in their respective nations. It was a devastating revelation, this secret pattern of contemporary Africa's self-proclaimed deliverers.

The essay's tremors jolted the president, who hated being exposed in a negative fashion to the outside world. This would only exacerbate the reluctance of foreign leaders to invite him to visit them, he thought. Leaders in Europe and North America who saw human rights as an article of faith would not even allow him into their countries. What a catastrophe! He was being put on the defensive. Every warrior, player, or gamester knows that offensive play yields victory. If you continue to defend yourself, what time do you have left to pull off victory or score any goals? He asked himself many rhetorical questions.

The cabinet and members of the Armed Forces Ruling Council (AFRC) met to discuss David Rupert's article. The court praise-singers railed against white people who liked to meddle especially in black people's affairs because they had no respect for Africans and their sovereignty. Why should white people still consider black people as babies that should be taken care of? The president's men pursued this line of attack that they knew most Africans would identify with. They presented their head as an African nationalist under siege because of his fierce determination to turn the country into a truly African State. Nobody knew what they meant by "a truly African State" but it was a weapon of defence and offense in General Ogiso's arsenal.

The government suspected Dede Daro but was not very sure if he was really the David Rupert. It would be too blatant a form of persecution to deal with him under the circumstances. With so many of the hungry lawyers now calling themselves human rights attorneys, any act against him would make them instant celebrities, which they sought to be, in order to have clients for other cases. Would the government prosecutors not look stupid to bring in witnesses to identify the black bearded and moustached Dede Daro as the same David Rupert who wrote the article? When have Urhobo men started to have Rupert as their family name? Who would identify him as his son, brother, nephew, or cousin? Some cases were better served if left alone than pursued. Whoever was seeking martyrdom would not be made one by the State, President Ogiso advised his cabinet.

Since there was none of its nationals called David Rupert, the government filed complaints to the American Embassy and *Time Magazine* respectively to ask American media to stop interfering in the internal affairs of a sovereign African nation. Several overzealous cabinet members took the matter as a political affront to which they had to respond in defence of their president and fatherland. Together they wrote an open letter to the President of the United States of America and bought a page each of *The New York Times* and *The Washington Post* at an exorbitant price to have the letter published.

Many months later Dede would realize how, despite his veiled identity, others would suffer innocently because of the essay that made him famous. He would become too toxic to come close to publicly and one person with whom he had mutual respect and love would die from it.

Despite the internal bruises of the broken marriage, Dede now held his head high and walked straight into his office. The office walls had greyed a little more than before, the paint peeling off and leaving the appearance of neglect. The early downpours of the rainy season had started and made the atmosphere cool and damp at the same time. Despite the many cleaners daily sweeping the place, there was dust on the office furniture and equipment. The buildings housing the offices and production line of *The African Patriot* stood by the busy Badagry Expressway. The heavy traffic of vehicles raised dust that easily settled on the newspaper's premises.

He had taken a month's leave when his case with Franka was raging. He felt it was the right thing to do; hence he explained his views to Ena Tobore, the publisher of *The African Patriot*, about the need to separate himself from the paper at that time. He had been separated from Franka for over six months before the two cases.

After the cases, he took another two weeks off to reflect on his life. Am I Janus, double-faced gateman of my society? Am I a human rights activist that they call me or am I inflicting inhuman rights on others? What am I? Will readers of my pieces remember my private life and be turned off? He asked himself many questions.

During the period of Dede's silent self-examination and withdrawal from the public, some rumoured he was writing a novel about the unborn leader of the nation. They said that he was reflecting on how that child would be conceived in the first place, with most of the men impotent and the women sterile or prostitutes and wondering, with the sick state of the nation, whether the baby would not be still-born, if born at all. Others gossiped that he had joined a cult whose members read the secret calligraphy of a spider's web and also communed silently with spirits behind closed doors. They knew that he always wanted to be in the limelight and had no other explanation for his silence and invisibility at the time. A parrot does not turn dumb without cause, more so as the public knows how vociferous it has always been.

He had been approached several months earlier to be the master of ceremony in a book launching ceremony and had accepted. He knew when the book was being written and the author had told him about the publishing arrangements. He wanted more than ever to prepare for the occasion. Since the telephone carrier, NITEL, announced that there were technical problems that would take weeks to fix, he had to drive to Ikeja to see Mrs. Eunice Fatumbi, the geography teacher at Akowe High School, to check on how far she had gone in the preparation for the launching of her geography textbook. He always enjoyed chatting with her when there was the opportunity, and both of them got carried away in their conversations.

Both had met a long time ago abroad when she was already engaged to a businessman at home. She was determined on returning home, as Dede also was. They had mutual admiration for each other. He, unlike the other men, remained friends with her after she made it known that she was engaged and that she was not interested in a romantic relationship. Franka had, for reasons unknown to him, not liked the woman's name mentioned in her presence. Now he had nobody to displease by going to see her.

8

Dede had taken his son, Uvie, who was in his care, to live with his mother right after the court case, almost as soon as he learned that Franka had sent Kena to her mother. It was purely a coincidence though, because he had already reasoned that the child would learn much more staying in a rural environment than in the city. But he had arrived at that decision after discovering, as soon as he had been given custody of the boy, that it was going to be a daunting task for him. He knew that his mother would not agree to come to live in Lagos to help look after Uvie. She had visited during the marriage crisis and taken Kena away only to bring her back for the court appearance. To her, Lagos was a place to visit and leave for one's permanent residence and not a place to settle in for life. She complained that there were too many cars and too much noise and so could not live there. He visited her every other month and he wanted to see her and Uvie again.

What he saw in his last visit gladdened his heart. Uvie already spoke Urhobo without stammering and had also learned some folktales and riddles. He even repeated a few tongue-twisters at a faster speed than he, an adult, could do. *Kua kp'Ekrebuo, kua kp'Ekrebuo, Ekrebuo b'ekua ra. Br'oke, br'oke, br'owho br'oke k'owho*! The boy was blending well with his school and playmates. This proper rooting of his child, as he saw it, gladdened his heart immensely. He felt it was right for him to go regularly to check on him and be assured that he was doing well and not missing both father and mother in such a way as to cause emotional problems in the child's life.

He had left his Datsun car to rest since it would be a punishing journey for it through the pot-holed roads from Lagos to Warri. That car needed comprehensive servicing to endure the long and tedious journey and that would cost much money that he could not now afford. There was also the problem of police extortion on the road. He wanted to avoid any confrontation with the police on the way.

Motor parks and bus stations were almost everywhere in Lagos, but Iddo was the largest of them and also the most reliable to get a vehicle going to one's destination at anytime of the day. He wound his way through the throng of people to the Warri section of the motor park, a section he was now familiar with. He wore a light blue safari shirt and a deep blue pair of trousers. He carried a brown briefcase and a folded brown garment bag. He believed in travelling light. When he asked for which taxi was next to travel to Warri, a middle-aged man, who was coincidentally the driver, pointed out a Peugeot station wagon to him.

A woman was already sitting in one of the middle seats in the taxi. He was pleasantly surprised that the sole passenger had not chosen the front seat. He opened the door to take the empty front passenger seat that was so coveted by travellers.

Once in, he turned back to greet the woman behind.

"Good morning, madam!"

She appeared startled, but quickly regained her composure.

"Good morning," she answered.

After a glance here and there, he soon settled down to read his copy of *Tell,* placing on his lap an assortment of the day's newspapers.

Outside, the taxi-driver was shouting "Warri! Sapele!" The same car took passengers to both towns; it dropped the Sapele passengers at a filling station at the outskirts of town and continued onward to Warri.

"Can I read your copy of *The Concord*?" the woman behind asked.

"Sure. Take it," and he passed her not only the *Concord* but also the *Observer* that he had gone through.

Each paper had its own reputation and he knew each one's ideology. He always wanted to read all the papers, but he knew that many were not worth the time because they only printed military decrees and so-called achievements. *The African Patriot* was new and radical, a consideration that brought him onboard.

He also observed his fellow passenger closely, as he raised his head to look at the people milling past that side of the motor park. She was beautifully shaped, he told himself. Her oval face with rather big warm eyes made her look very different from the women he saw around. Her face carried a certain mystique though. It was languorous and calm, yet at the same time appeared perturbed beneath.

"I am Dede. And you?"

"Furu," she answered.

"What a lovely-sounding name you have, Furu!"

"And yours too. Dede sounds beautiful."

Furu's voice had a soft musicality to it, as if she was a singer.

She had bought both *The Guardian* and *The African Patriot* when she first arrived, hoping to while away the time before the taxi filled up. Instead, she folded the papers without reading them, and placed them on her lap. She had other things occupying her mind.

Furu was leaving Lagos for home almost in a hurry. She had to cut short what she had planned to be a long visit. She must leave Lagos, she had told herself the past night. She had gone to the beach in Victoria Island the previous evening in the company of her friends. That was her third time there. After the earlier two visits, she felt going alone to see the pastor was neither prudent nor safe. He had asked her on each visit to spend the night with him so that he could pray for her. The pastor, a clean-shaven and white-robed middle-aged man, was playing a hawk-and-chicken game with her, and she had to avoid being alone with him.

"I don't sleep outside my home," she told him.

"Big woman like you no fit sleep outside? You no be pickin," the preacher had responded.

"Yes, but that's the way I have been brought up to live."

"You wan tell me say you never do am or wetin?" he asked.

"Do wetin?" Furu asked, as if she didn't understand the sexual overtone of the pastor's words.

"Think about it," he said as he slipped into the holy of holies, the comfortably furnished annex to the altar that Prophet Jeremiah retreated to after turning his congregation into a frenzied mood.

There, his congregation believed, he dialogued with God over their problems. They heard him speak a language they did not understand, indistinct blabbering, but which they believed was a spiritual tongue. Every service came to a crescendo with the prophet speaking in tongues followed by a drum sequence accompanied with delirious dance.

Prophet Jeremiah felt that the few testimonies Furu had witnessed would make her open up to him. It was going to be a slow but gradual process, softening her into submission. Many women before her had started the same way, unwilling to be possessed by the Holy Spirit or him the representative, but had with time thrown their bodies at him. He expected Furu to do the same. If huge stones could be rolled, what woman would not be moved out of her frigid self? he asked himself.

"This na modern world. Abi, you think say you still dey Stone Age?" he asked Furu, just as he came back from his inner sanctum.

"You be pastor or wetin you be?" she asked back.

That blunt question weakened the pastor's resolve and gave her space to escape his net.

She had gone back to the beach church because she saw for herself the middle-aged women with their first babies. Word of mouth had spread the news that it was Prophet Jeremiah who prayed for them to have babies at their age. It was not just hearsay, those rather old women carrying their own babies for the first time and dancing deliriously in the church. Only the prayers of a pastor who dialogued with God could make women almost past their menopause to conceive. Only a powerful pastor, a prayer-warrior, could pull off the miracle of the five old women and their five babies.

And so Furu nursed the hope that what had worked for those women after so many years of marriage would also work for her. But for the pastor to invite her into the church's inner room in a faked trance and to whisper into her ears that he could impregnate her, if she was willing, was a shocking experience. *Is this what happens in the new churches? Were those five women impregnated by the prophet or their husbands? Won't it be revealing to check whether those babies were Prophet Jeremiah's children?* Furu asked herself many questions that she knew only God could answer.

Up till now, the bells and drums that accompanied the voice of the prophet in a wave-breaking alto in the Beach Church of Christ last night had continued to rebound in her head.

Furu was still daydreaming when Dede boarded the taxi. Now she had landed in reality again, though still perplexed about her life, even as she read the papers.

Soon the driver and his tout had dragged another traveller to the car. The man was suspicious as he appeared used to the trickery of touts sitting in the car pretending to be passengers, only to leave as one or two real travellers came in. Many travellers had to make sure that they were not being deceived before going in. The man tore himself off their grip immediately when he saw Dede.

"Hi, Dede!" he exclaimed.

"Hi, Tori," he answered.

Furu stared at them. They were so excited; they must have been close at one time, she thought.

"Seven years! Yes, seven years. I heard you've been back," Dede said.

"Yes, these Oke people are still persecuting me. I have to take them to court," Tori told him.

41

"Take them to court for what reason?" he asked.

"They are still keeping me down," Tori explained.

He was used to Tori's stories about his experience in the civil service in Lagos. While studying at Syracuse University, Tori always lambasted the tribalism of the majority groups. He had argued many years ago that his Oke superiors in the office had sent him on study-leave with pay for four years and to come back with automatic promotion to the next scale because they wanted to get rid of him.

"I may have to leave the service," he told Dede.

"Leave for what?" he asked.

"If only to leave this tribalistic civil service for private practice," he answered, laughing incoherently.

"Of course, that's what every retiree does nowadays. Return to private practice, after making too much money to continue working," he teased him.

"Dede, you know that these wicked people with whom I work will never allow me to retire with a penny. I wish there were more of us minorities to fight them," he sighed.

Tori had entered the civil service as a clerical officer and risen with only his secondary school certificate to a senior executive officer before his study-leave abroad.

"Dede, where are you travelling to?" Tori asked

"Warri," he told him.

"I am going to Warri too," he said. "But how much is the fare?" he asked.

"Five hundred naira," he answered.

"Five hundred naira!" Tori shouted with disbelief. "Am I flying abroad?" he asked loudly.

"These fares increase by the day. It is a pity we have no control over what these drivers charge," Dede told him.

"Let me go and look for a place to ease myself. If the car fills up before I come back, go. We'll meet in Warri," Tori said, dragging his bag away and soon disappearing into the crowd.

After reading the papers, Furu gave them back to Dede. Both passengers were quiet for some time, but soon laughed simultaneously as a *kolo* man performed obscene antics in front of their car. After the madman left for another car, Dede decided to change his seat. He moved to the right-hand seat of the middle row. He and Furu were now together in the same row and could talk to each other from close proximity.

The car finally filled up and the passengers paid their fares. Furu moved to the middle seat, directly to Dede's left. An elderly man had come in and she gave up the side seat to him for the less comfortable middle seat. The journey would have been faster had it not been for the police; their many checkpoints were there for the driver to contend with. It appeared he knew many of the policemen, who waved him to pass once they recognized who he was. He told his passengers that his senior brother was a police inspector and those on the road knew that; hence they passed him. He said he still gave the police tips now and then because his brother's position in the police force was not enough to free him all the time from the greed of those on the highway.

The driver stopped at Ofosu, as was customary in the long journey, for his passengers to eat, stretch, or go to relieve themselves. Many women beckoned them to their respective restaurants, praising their foods as the best around. You could smell different spices but would not be able to tell where they came from. Furu asked Dede if he liked fresh fish and *banga* soup, to which he replied "Of course, that's my favourite dish." The two went to the farthest shed, which Furu knew prepared the best *banga* soup around.

Dede's hair was low-cut. He was one of those who did not believe in visiting the barber too often, not only because it was time-consuming, but also because he wanted to be a little rough in his appearance. He wore a short beard and a moustache that fitted his face very well. He did not allow them to be bushy though to avoid Ogiso's ire.

Furu wore a head-tie, which did not hide her deep black braided hair. Her large Africa-shaped earrings dangled from side to side when she moved. She was gap-toothed. She did not talk much. Dede was used to interviewing people and he had asked her many questions. Within the past three hours, he knew that she was a teacher in an elementary school in Warri and liked the children she taught a lot. He, without her prompting, told her he was a journalist. It was at this time that she recalled having heard his name mentioned before.

After the meal, he was satisfied that they had gone to the right place. He offered to pay, but she objected and insisted that she would pay her share. She then brought out some perfume from her handbag and asked him to open his palms, which she sprayed with a most pleasing scent. They went back to the car when the driver blew the horn to summon his passengers to continue the journey to Warri, which was still more than two and a half hours away. Within another five minutes of the driver's call, they took off. The road was filled with large and deep potholes and the driver had to meander around them. The car bumped the passengers now to one side and then to another. The tar on many parts of the road had peeled off. The supposedly dual carriageway had

43

one side closed and all cars used the same side. Those coming from the wrong direction flashed their lights at those on the right side trying to intimidate them to give them more space to drive through.

There were many police checkpoints before Benin. At a point the driver had to suddenly clamp down the brakes to avoid running over a tree trunk across his side of the road. Beyond it, the police had placed a big plank with big nails so that any driver that passed the tree trunk would be forced to stop with punctured tires from the nails. The car almost somersaulted but the driver's experience helped him to steady the steering and to remain on the road. After the police queried the driver for not driving slowly and smoothly, they called him aside and released him after hushed transactions behind the car's raised bonnet.

The roadside villages bustled with activities. Placed by the road for display and sale were bags of *garri*, yams, plantain, snails, fresh vegetables, and fruits. Between the villages lay stretches of impenetrable lush rain forest.

It took the car one hour to go through Benin. The main streets were flooded and many cars and buses were abandoned on the waterlogged roads. The driver took several diversions to get to the Benin-Sapele Road. At one point, he pointed at a spot where he had been held up by armed robbers the previous week. Two of his passengers were robbed of hundreds of thousands of naira. Armed robbery was done in Benin with such precision as found nowhere else in the country, the driver said.

Dede and Furu talked more familiarly as they came closer to Warri. They could observe that the drivers were very fast compared to what they had seen earlier. She realized that the slogan of Warri drivers going to Benin at top speed was "Benin by air!" The cars were flying on the road.

They exchanged addresses in the hope of communicating with each other. At the Warri motor park, before parting, they held each other's hand in a handshake.

"Nice meeting you," he told her.

"Thanks. Nice meeting you too," she replied.

"Bye!"

"Bye!"

When he looked back after a few steps, he realized that she had also turned back and their eyes met; they smiled and waved at each other again before leaving for their separate destinations in town.

In Okpara Dede was just Daro's son living in Lagos. The small townspeople knew that he now made a living from writing, their understanding of a journalist's career, but did not know the extent of his popularity or renown. He enjoyed his homeboy status, as the elders still saw him as a young man. They were happy when he went abroad on a scholarship to study.

"Great Agbon!" they had chanted in celebration.

"Great Okpara!" others had chanted.

"Okpara always elevates!" they had chorused.

"I knew he would go very far," Uncle Tobi boasted to his townsmen, after his spattering of Dede's childhood recitation of *Friends, Romans, and countrymen.*

Many of their sons and daughters were very intelligent and they saw Dede Daro following the line of those gone abroad. No other clan around was like Agbon and no other town like Okpara produced such intelligent young ones who went overseas to study. Some had been abroad for dozens of years, working and studying, they boasted.

They were surprised and rather disappointed when Dede returned from overseas within only two years and said that he was not a lawyer or a doctor but a newspaperman. They felt his journey to the white man's land was wasted, since one did not need to go that far to learn to be a newspaperman. When they learnt that he had gone to study in the United States of America rather than in England, they exclaimed, "No wonder!" Most of their children who wrote them that they were studying law and medicine were not returning from abroad and the few returning already old had gone to England. America was a different place, they realized. Unfazed by his American education, Uncle Tobi still addressed his Okpara townsfolks as *Friends, Romans, and countrymen.*

Dede returned early the following day from Okpara, after seeing his parents and son. He went straight to ask for Furu at Igbudu Primary School, one of the oldest schools in Warri and beside the Warri River as it leaves town, undulating towards Effurun. When a female typist from the headmaster's office came to tell her that a man was looking for her, she wondered who that would be. In all the years she had been in the school, she had not once received a male visitor. Was her friend coming back to make up for his indifference? Or who else could that man be? Dede did not come to her mind. She was therefore very surprised to see him but felt pleased. He told her that he felt like seeing her again before going back to Lagos the following day. They agreed to meet in the early evening at River Valley Hotel, where he was staying.

She came as they had arranged. They went to the garden and sat on benches set for outdoor lovers. It was breezy and cool, the sort of weather after the downpour the previous night. Dede called one of the service boys to bring soft drinks. He had known from their table conversation at Ofusu that Furu did not take alcohol.

He talked about his newspaper work that took him out sometimes without adequate notice. But he liked having a family to return to after being out chasing or investigating news.

"There's nothing like being welcomed home," he said.

"Sure, there's nothing like company," she told him.

She confessed she had a friend, who had of late become lukewarm to her. She had already set her mind on ending the relationship and had told the man that neither of them could go on at that rate. The man had said, "If that's what pleases you!" A man in love with a woman would not say any such thing to her, she said.

She also told Dede how her marriage of twelve years was mutually dissolved because she could not conceive all those years. He saw the contrast between her divorce, which was amicably settled traditionally, and his bitter divorce in a magistrate court.

On his side, he explained that he had come to Delta State to see his five-year old son, Uvie, who was with his parents in Okpara. He was newly divorced and was thinking about what to do with the rest of his life.

After talking about themselves, they talked about Warri of the past with its swashbuckler *boma* boys and vibrant night clubs now all gone. So were the cinema houses that showed American and Indian films that brought much excitement to the young people all gone.

"I see the ghosts of boma boys whenever I come to Warri," he said.

"And of the crowds from the cinema houses," she added.

They knew when Warri was in vogue, there was so much excitement for all its residents. But Warri had changed to a crowded city without the social events that made it so appealing and famous.

The moon was rising from the western horizon and stars were taking their positions on the wide sky. Dede escorted Furu to the road to take a taxi home.

9

Dede came back to Lagos with Mrs. Eunice Fatumbi's book launch on his mind. Rather, the woman he always had so much praise for was on his mind. Mrs. Fatumbi had her BS and MS in Geography from Vassar College, New York, where she was on the Dean's List every semester and proved that she more than deserved the scholarship with which she had entered the school.

He liked Mrs. Fatumbi. To him, a beautiful and intelligent woman who had committed all her resources to the academic improvement of the nation's youths should be fully supported. A woman who could forego the latest fashions in expensive "dressing-to-match" materials to write an ambitious textbook for secondary school students should be applauded.

Five years of preparation of this geography book was a period of constant sacrifice. All her savings from the United States went into it. She did not bring back many of the luxuries that academic returnees brought back from New York or London. Her monthly savings from her earnings the past several years amounted to a good sum, but still not enough to cover the one and a half million naira cost of the two hundred thousand copies of her book.

She received no financial support from her husband who was always on the road as a contractor. Though he was a good provider for domestic needs, he was not doing as well as he would make people believe. He spent more time pursuing payments of completed projects than seeking new contracts. Both respected each other's call. She had been engaged to him when she visited home during one of her vacations. She had remained faithful during the years she was alone in the United States and had beaten off many tempting proposals from her countrymen studying abroad who were knocked out by her beauty and affable personality. She had first met Dede when she was already engaged at an Independence Day party at the Nigerian Mission in New York and they had liked each other since their meeting. She kept her promise, returned and married Mr. Fatumbi.

A coloured textbook was a rarity in the nation's schools; there was none in geography before this. The book featured many coloured photographs of humans in their cultural, social, and economic settings. Mrs. Fatumbi believed that boys and girls learn more from what they can see and hear. In this case, colour would be an incentive for them to grasp the geographical experience of their region.

The publisher, Akin, had excitedly volunteered to "chip in" nine hundred thousand naira. His company was not rich and not doing well but he believed he had to take risks if the fortunes of his publishing house must improve drastically. He suspected his new author did not know she had struck a gold mine with a much-needed and groundbreaking textbook. He expected to make a huge profit from his investment in *The Human Geography of West Africa* to turn upwards the fortunes of his company.

The Principal of Akowe High School, who liked to be called "Provost", coughed out one hundred thousand naira. The amount was taken from the school's discretionary funds and given as a loan to an industrious staff. He had no doubt that Mrs. Fatumbi would get a windfall from the launching and sale of the book. Paying back the loan would be no problem, he judged. And there was the expectation of the West African Examinations Council adopting his teacher's book as a recommended text. Apart from making his private school famous and the desire of every family to send their children there, this project could make millionaires of not only the writer and publisher, but the patrons as well with its success.

The few books published in the country at the time sold out as soon as they were launched. Mrs. Fatumbi was realistic enough to know her limits. She did not have the clout of a First Lady whose **Home Front** raised fifty million naira at its launching. Nor did she have the talent to sing the praises of the military regime in the newspapers—an easy way of gaining recognition and government appointments and favours.

The Art Mistress of Akowe High School, popularly known as Mrs. Toyin, specially designed the invitation card. She objected to Dede Daro's name being boldly displayed on the card that would be sent all over the country.

"I don't like this Frank Dede of a person to be publicly associated with you," she told Mrs. Fatumbi.

"His name is Dede Daro, not Frank Dede," she corrected.

The author realized that the tabloid reporting on Dede's divorce and custody cases had done the distortion in the public's mind to such an extent that he was now called Frank Dede.

"Why, my dear?" she asked back.

"You know this our country. Government is the provider for all and nobody wants to annoy it. Frank Dede, I beg your pardon, Dede Daro and Government don't agree," Mrs. Toyin explained.

Nobody knew why she was called Mrs. Toyin. Toyin was her first name, but somehow she did not protest being called Mrs. Toyin. Her family name of Ajala went virtually ignored by those who knew her. She wore a ring on her right forefinger, but nobody believed she was married.

"But he is a brilliant journalist," the author insisted.

"Yes, but the launching is business and I don't want anybody to pour sand into your carefully prepared pot of soup. In this country, people eat forbidden foods and wipe their mouths so as not to be caught," Mrs.Toyin told her. "You may like or respect him, but you don't have to let people see you with him in public or associated with your name on an important invitation card," she continued.

"Is it because of the David Rupert article they suspect he wrote against the government?" Mrs. Fatumbi asked.

"Of course, yes. No government official or contractor would want to appear on television or in the newspaper sitting at a function with Frank Dede, please forgive me, Dede Daro, the no-nonsense journalist. But it all depends on you. It is your book, not mine," she conceded.

"I have to keep to my word with him. I approached him a long time ago to be the MC, and he agreed. He has all along been following the writing of this book and has done his best to encourage me to where I am today. I want the book launching, apart from raising money to cover the production costs, to be a meeting of minds," Mrs. Fatumbi said in defence of her preferred choice of an MC.

"I hope the chief launcher, the publisher, and other invitees will enjoy this meeting of minds with Dede," Mrs. Toyin said, knowing she could not sway Mrs. Fatumbi from her steadfast faith in Dede.

The beautifully glossy invitation cards flew into every corner of Lagos and the country. Mrs. Fatumbi had a committee to provide her names of those to be invited.

"You must be inviting the whole world," Mrs.Toyin told her.

"It will be an opportunity to bring people together and highlight the importance of human geography in our national development," she explained.

"Are you going to put them in a house or a football field?" Mrs.

Toyin asked in her mischievous manner.

"At the National Theatre's Main Auditorium," she replied.

"I know that, but the place does not need to be filled with people," the Art teacher told her friend.

"Since there's plenty of space for people, why can't I invite as many people interested in education as possible?" Mrs. Fatumbi asked.

"I hope you didn't have to take a loan for it. It will be a big crowd to serve drinks and snacks. Our people are fond of drinking and eating more than they donate. I won't be surprised if many of your invitees only drink and eat and do not buy your book," Mrs. Toyin told her.

The two teachers were friends, but the married woman kept the single Toyin at some distance. Toyin was the devil's advocate that she knew she sometimes needed.

"You know, Toyin, that everything from the writing to the publishing and launching of this book is being done through loans," the author confided in her friend.

"May God help you," Toyin said in prayer.

The eve of the launching, Mrs. Fatumbi went to bed late in her attempt to put finishing touches to the arrangements. She had long dreams at short intervals. In one such dream, cows pursued her, and she ran fast into a house that opened to her but was policed by huge dogs that barked at her ferociously. She was surprised that she could run so fast in spite of her pregnancy.

In another dream, rain beat her over a long stretch but she did not get wet. But the dream that bothered her most was the one in which she was dancing vigorously without being pregnant and everybody was clapping for her. She did not believe in dreams like Mrs. Toyin who had told her that she went to consult a *babalawo* when she had bad dreams. But she was uncomfortable, as she was more tired at dawn than before she went to bed. Dawn, at last, brought the much-awaited day.

Mrs. Fatumbi arrived at the National Theatre at 8 a.m. though the place was already arranged. She wanted the event to happen without a hitch. She had made copies of her one-page speech. She opted for a short speech because she wanted the content of the book to speak for itself. She also wanted to give time to the MC, Dede Daro, the reviewer, and the chief launcher to do the talking.

Dede arrived at 9:30 a.m., thinking he had come very early but still found Mrs. Fatumbi already there and sweating from cleaning the already cleaned floor and re-arranging the already arranged chairs. It was still more than one hour before the start of the event.

"Madam Early Bird, you're already here," Dede teased her.

"Of course DD, I should be an early bird this day of all days," she answered in a rather weak voice.

"I hope you slept well?" he asked, noticing the feeble voice of a constantly vibrant woman.

"Not as well as I would have liked to. It was a short and restless sleep, touch-and-go sort of sleep filled with many dreams," she told him.

"Don't be too anxious," he said.

"Is your speech ready?" she asked.

"It's ready. Just five pages! I have made about five hundred copies for the important dignitaries."

"Will that number be enough?" she asked.

"That should be sufficient. I cannot give copies to everybody in attendance. If I do that, soon one has to prepare copies for everybody in the country and that will be a lot. Only those who are likely to donate money or buy the book and the pressmen and women really need copies. I don't need to give copies to those who would not read the speech. At least they will hear it," he told her.

"You know these procedures better than I do. I am really a novice in book-launching," she said.

They laughed. She became a little more relaxed. She enjoyed Dede's company and felt he was perhaps the only person in town who truly understood her and her work. Until the publishing of the book, almost all her colleagues at Akowe High School had dismissed her effort as a waste of time. The women teachers in particular did not see the need for such a beautiful and very educated woman to suffer, as they saw it, to make money. There were many effortless ways of making money in Lagos and enjoying herself upon it all if she was smart. She disliked them and rarely had a meaningful conversation with them. The few times Dede visited her, they talked about what enriched her soul, as she admitted to him. She would like them to chat more often but both of them were busy people. She had gone to see him in his office only once and they had chatted till late before she left. With him as the MC, she had every reason to believe that things would go on very well at the launching.

At eleven, when the ceremony was due to start, none of the invitees had come.

"When will we learn to be punctual?" Mrs. Fatumbi asked Dede.

"You don't know that not being clock-punctual is an African disease?" he asked back.

"Even to an important occasion like this?"

"Of course, yes. They like to take their time. Can't you see how far we are behind the rest of the world?" he asked back.

"I hate this African time," she said loudly, as if she was talking to many people and scolding them.

"The leopard, you know, cannot shed its spots. The spots make it what it is," he said.

Akowe High School's principal, the "Provost", came in dressed in overflowing "up-and- down" robes. His driver carried his brown brief case and followed him like a personal servant and guard. From his flamboyant appearance, he looked more like a businessman than a high school principal.

"The place is still empty like this?" he queried, as if he had sent chauffeurs in cars he provided to bring the invitees to the venue of the ceremony.

"They have not yet come," Mrs. Fatumbi said feebly.

By 11:30 a.m. the publisher, his sales manager, and public relations officer came in. They had expected to come into an already filled hall. The publisher shook his head at the empty seats. He shook hands with the principal and the art teacher and sat beside them.

It soon came to 12:00 noon. The waiting was silent and cheerless. The big clock on the wall began to tick loudly as if it had just started working. The light in the hall slightly dimmed in direct response to the sun outside slipping into dark clouds. There was uneasiness in the atmosphere in the hall that none present would articulate, as if doing so would doom the ceremony.

As time passed, the wall clock's monotonous tick-tock rhythm became irritating to Mrs. Fatumbi. She walked over to the far end of the hall to sit, her head bowed down. She closed her eyes, hoping she would open them to see the place transformed into a crowd. Once, twice, and thrice she tried it to no avail. She could not conjure up people to fill up the hall. *What is keeping people at home or on the road that they have not yet arrived here? If there is no traffic jam this Saturday morning, what is holding them back? What is stopping their cars from starting?* Her mind was asking itself many questions.

One o'clock arrived. Two whole hours after the occasion was supposed to have started! The chief launcher, the chairman of the national association of secondary school principals, Dr. Bruce Jide, had not even arrived. His selection as chief launcher was informed by Mrs. Fatumbi's desire to have an academic event and he had reassured her that he would be there to open the launching with a hefty sum.

Dede Daro, as the master of ceremony, doubted if the date was correct. He looked at his watch and it read the correct day. He looked out for Mrs. Fatumbi, who was at the other end of the empty hall, her head on the table. He went to her.

"Let's postpone it," he told her.

Somehow both of them knew without saying it that Dede Daro's name, emblazoned on the invitation card, had apparently caused the failed launching. The toxic fallout of David Rupert's essay!

Both went to join others sitting together but not talking to one another.

"We have to call it off. We can't launch this book today. If today were April 1 and not August 1, I would have felt it was a fools' day," Dede told them.

It was a bright day, quite unlike some days the previous week that were drowned in floods. The August Break, true to its nature and name, was just beginning. The earlier dark and gray clouds that covered the sky had all disappeared and left the sky one bright silver roof from where the sun shot its arrows of light.

10

On her return from Lagos, Furu went to see her mother at Egbo. She told her about her experiences during the trip to the big city, except her meeting with Dede. She wanted to satisfy herself that if she became his friend, she was not having two men at the same time, a practice she did not like and also knew very well her mother would frown at. The former relationship was over and fortunately in time for her to start her life afresh at thirty-five.

For several months her real lover had been a succubus that pressed her at night. Always, as soon as she fell asleep, he came from nowhere to mount her. It was so real that many times she felt she was awake and really making love. But the succubus was a faceless male, whose body features she could not see. In every instance, she could not throw him off her body till it was too late. On several occasions, the faceless figure penetrated her and she had an orgasm, which she surprisingly enjoyed and wished had lasted much longer.

When she told her mother about the recurring strange experience, the old woman chuckled and told her that the earth needed rain to flourish; hence they were good friends. She wondered what the statement meant.

"You are no longer a small girl," her mother told her.

"I don't need to be told that," she responded.

"Yes, I know you are no longer a child but you are still very far from old age, my daughter. A fallow field needs to be cultivated. Of course, an empty market invites spirits," her mother said.

"But I have seen men and don't want them," she told her mother.

"You are still a child then. Your womanhood desires fulfilment. You need a man," she advised her.

At school Furu put in her best to help the pupils, some of whom were well-behaved and the others not. She was friendly with her fellow teachers, but none of them could be called a close friend. Occasionally they talked, but everybody appeared to be self-absorbed in looking for ways to make money.

Some weekends, after returning from the market, she felt lonely. She would have liked company, but making friends in Warri was difficult. The men wanted you just for sex and abandoned you as soon as another woman, usually a younger one, caught their fancy. As for the women, they gossiped a lot. Women friends also encouraged unnecessary competition in dressing to social occasions such as weddings, burial ceremonies, and parties that were plentiful. She would not be able to cope with women who saw their lives as only dressing to impress men. She would live her life outside such circles.

Dede and Furu exchanged letters regularly. Both hoped a time would come for one to visit the other. And that would happen sooner than either anticipated.

He invited her for a weekend in Lagos and she accepted. She liked him and wanted to know more about him and she knew that he also wanted to know more about her. The initial date for the visit was changed because her school had an inter-house sports' competition and she had to be around to officiate with other teachers. Fortunately, the mid-term break was approaching and, if she wanted, could spend more time than just two days in Lagos.

As Dede prepared for Furu's visit, he was distraught by the recent tragedy that had taken place. He couldn't believe that Mrs. Eunice Fatumbi was dead. *She was the only woman I could relate to comfortably. She was lively, intelligent, and beautiful. I loved her and she knew I did. I think she also loved me and knew I knew that. However, our particular circumstances kept us restrained. My good friend has died. Eunice, farewell!* He felt partly responsible for her death—the toxic fallout of the Rupert essay. But apportioning blame for her death, he realized, would not bring her back to life. *What a loss!*

The school teacher-author had been taken to hospital the evening following the abortive book launching. She complained of severe headaches and blurred vision. It was a rather mysterious case because the doctor was not able to determine what was wrong with her; he ran blood tests, but the results gave him no lead to follow to treat her. He ordered her to just rest as he tried to consult his colleagues to figure out what was wrong with her.

Even when in hospital, the publisher came to her to complain about the money he had invested in the book. Nine hundred thousand naira was a huge sum that a small publishing house in dire straits could not afford to lose if it wanted to remain alive. Akin had thought the huge investment would resuscitate his failing company, but instead, without the money paid back, the company would be totally ruined.

The publisher thought about ways of salvaging his sinking ship and was sleepless for several days. He became more agitated the more he thought about the failed book launching. He needed to do something for himself and his company, and concluded that business demanded toughness. The man who used to be clean-shaven and flamboyantly dressed looked unkempt. He wore what should be a three-piece outfit, but without the cap.

The failed launching had been compounded by the fact that there was no possibility now that the book would be adopted for secondary school use.

"I will be finished, my company will be bankrupt. What I have laboured for all my life will be ruined," he screamed at the blank-faced Mrs. Fatumbi.

He might as well be screaming at the wall. The publisher noticed that his author's medical condition was very bad and that drove him into a delirious rage. When he started to brandish a copy of the book like a machete at the patient, the attending nurse felt she had endured enough of the madman's harangues. She summoned her energy and pushed Mr. Akin, who fell on the floor. Everybody around stared at him as if he were a lunatic who should be pitied. On the ground he started to stammer some words. The nurse grasped one of the poles that held the drip like a shield. Everybody expected the madman to charge at the nurse or at the patient, but the publisher gave a long look at Mrs. Fatumbi in her sick bed, got up, and began to walk away.

The pregnant woman had to remain in the hospital for a week, instead of the few days earlier anticipated, for observation. With sedatives, she slept well and the doctor felt she could rest at home to fully regain her health before going back to her job.

Upon her discharge, there was a long letter from her publisher waiting for her. It was placed on her pillow and as soon as she was back, she saw the typed letter that she knew very well came from her publisher. She went on to read it.

"There is no way you will have peace after ruining my life. My workers and my family depend on me. You must be the worst woman on earth, a cankerworm that needs to be expunged from the environment. You are too conceited to be intelligent, too clever to be marketable in any meaningful way. You are just a loser." The letter rattled on and on.

She could not sleep all night. She turned from one side to another, but no sleep came to her. By the next morning, barely twelve hours after her discharge, she suffered a relapse and had to be rushed back to hospital late in the afternoon. By night she was dead. The baby also could not be saved. The nurses present said it was a massive stroke. But it was one of those cases of very sad demise that people did not ask about the cause of death. She was gone after all.

Before one month was over, both Mr. Akin and Mr. Fatumbi had sued each other. The publisher sued the author's husband, who had not been involved in the book business, asking for the company's expenditure of nine hundred thousand naira to be paid to him.

Soon Mr. Fatumbi got advice from unsolicited sources and had to sue Mr. Akin and his publishing house to compensate him for his wife's death. He asked the court to award him the amount of nine hundred thousand naira.

It did not come as a surprise when the court registrar, without their consent, merged the two cases into one.

The papers had a field day.

PUBLISHER MAD AFTER MYSTERIOUS DEATH OF FEMALE AUTHOR

A famous book publisher has gone mental after the failure of an expensive project and the imminent collapse of his company. Banks are threatening to seize his company's premises and his personal house where he lives with his family. The imminent prospect of being homeless and seeking shelter under one of the overhead bridges has taken a heavy toll on the man. He was stopped from setting his office on fire and his family members are closely watching his strange behaviour of talking to himself and addressing invisible creditors.

JOURNALIST BOTCHED BOOK LAUNCHING AND LEAVES BEHIND DEATH AND CLAIM SUITS

A popular journalist (name withheld) has ruined a book launching and left in its trail a stream of sorrow. The writer killed herself when nobody bought her book at the largely ignored launching. After her boast to her colleagues that she would be acclaimed a better writer than Wole Soyinka or Chinua Achebe, she could not bring herself to look anybody in the face anymore. The first day she went to school, her colleagues and students jeered at her. She told herself that enough was enough. And the rest has become a tragic story. . .

MAN WRANGLES WITH DEAD WIFE'S LOVERS

The husband of a deceased beautiful Lagos secondary school teacher takes his dead wife's lovers to court for adultery and murder. One of the lovers, a publisher, has joined the increasing number of lunatics in the city. His is the worst type since he is not under any of the bridges but permanently camped by a dump pit which he lives on. The husband of the woman had tried diabolic means to eliminate his wife's secret lovers. After he had got one of the lovers, the other one, a journalist, has been so scared that he has gone into hiding for fear of being killed. . .

Mrs. Toyin was paid by several papers that sent their writers to interview her and to make her corroborate what they wanted to write to please their scandal-loving readers.

"I told her from the start that that name should be removed," she told one of her interviewers.

"Why did she not listen to you?" the female editor asked.

"She believed too much in herself and the worth of intelligence. She told me that the journalist was a very intelligent man and should be gainfully employed rather than be left to write scathing articles against the government. I believe she loved him too because they held hands when he visited her at school," Mrs. Toyin confided in her.

"How do you know that?" the journalist asked.

"She was always praising him for one thing or another. And they first met in America. Who knows how close they were before she married? He came often to the school and both of them talked for hours and nobody knew what they discussed and laughed about. That was the only man who talked familiarly with her. And she called him DD; whatever that meant. You can tell that they shared some past moments nobody knows about together. She broke the journalist's marriage," Mrs. Toyin revealed.

"How true is that assertion?"

"She was my friend and I know when a married woman is secretly in love with another man. You could see it in both of them," she said.

"And what a sad fate, dying in that illicit love affair!" the interviewer concluded.

That year's story contest should be a very competitive one, and what had been dubbed "the book case" had provided materials and opportunities for many contestants.

11

Dede had not thought that after separating from Franka and the many months of living alone that he could ever be so excited because of a woman. But there he was, restless; his mind always fixed on Furu. After sending her his photograph, he asked her for hers, which he framed beautifully and hung on his bedroom wall. She was more than splendid in the traditional attire of wrapper, blouse, and head-tie stylishly worn.

The first Delta Line car to arrive in Lagos from Warri that day came into the station at 1 p.m. Furu was in it. As she stepped out, she saw Dede waving and coming towards her. They embraced and greeted each other warmly, before he went to take her bag to his car. He had washed his car to make it look nice despite its age.

"How was the journey?" he asked.

"Smooth and comfortable," she replied.

"I hope you had no police harassment," he said.

"There was none. The policemen leave the government-owned cars alone," she explained.

"I am happy you are here, and happy that you had a good journey," he told her.

"Thank you," she responded.

The chronic traffic jams of Lagos roads kept them en route for another hour. The early morning rain that day had exacerbated a bad situation. Drivers honked their horns, as if doing so would open up the clogged roads. Despite the madness, the cars crawled at a millipede speed towards their destinations.

At his home Dede showed her round the flat that she would live in for the next few days. The chairs were relatively new and comfortable because Franka had insisted three years earlier that the very old ones be replaced. He had then complained of needless extravagance that he was being subjected to. The same battle had been fought and won by Franka before a new rug was bought only two years ago. Now he cherished the furniture, which he did his best to bring to a beautiful shine for Furu's visit.

They kept each other awake with recollections of their childhood and their separate experiences. As they talked on and on, they did not realize how far night had gone until there was a cockcrow, a rare thing in Lagos. It was already past four o'clock.

They had barely slept three hours when a strange knock on the door woke them. The knock was hard and loud. It sounded as if the person knocking was desperately trying to get into the house, perhaps escaping from chasing dogs or robbers. There was a kick on the door and a loud shout followed.

"Are you hiding from me, Mr. Daro? I am Akin."

Dede recognized the publisher's voice but was surprised that he chose such an early morning hour to bother him with his complaints.

"Just wait, I'll open the door for you," he shouted from inside.

He went back to the bedroom to wear a shirt. As he came back, there was a bang on the door.

"I've seen you. Open the door for me!" Akin shouted as he fumbled with the doorknob.

Though he felt something was amiss, Dede knew opening the door fast would be better than delaying. Furu had got up and followed him to the door. When the door opened, they could see from Akin's bloodshot eyes, unkempt hair, and rattled appearance that there was trouble.

"Come in," Dede told him, as he gave him way to enter.

"No, I will not enter your house until this case is settled," he shouted, as if the person he was talking to was not beside him.

He dug his feet by the threshold and refused to move.

"Do you know how I can get a copy of the woman's American certificate?" he asked.

Dede knew that he was referring to Mrs. Fatumbi.

"I don't know anything about her certificate," he answered.

"I went to the Records Office and got her death certificate; that will do. Whatever earlier one her husband got, mine is as good as his," he blurted.

Dede almost asked what he was going to do with Mrs. Fatumbi's American or death certificate, but restrained himself because he knew that Akin was not in his right mind. He must have bribed somebody in the Records Office in Yaba to get him a death certificate.

"You are not of any help, but let me see you in court on Monday morning," Akin said, and turned to go.

It was Saturday morning.

Furu accompanied Dede to court on Monday morning. Mr. Fatumbi was already in the courtroom by the time they arrived. They greeted him and then went to sit on a different side of the courtroom. They glanced round for Akin, but he was not yet in the courtroom.

The Akin-Fatumbi double case was the third on the docket. The first two cases went very fast and by nine-thirty there was the call for the next case.

"The next case is the Book Case," the judge announced.

He adjusted his milk-white wig and smoothed his black gown. He was a short, fat man in his fifties. He bent down to write for a few minutes and, when finished, whispered to one of the court's policemen.

"Mr. Akin!" shouted the police.

There was no response to the call. A moment of silence followed.

"Mr. Fatumbi!" the court police shouted.

"Yes!" he responded.

He walked to the dock, his lawyer by his side. He had prepared for possible questions and was confident his lawyer would present his case in a persuasive manner.

The judge started to write again. He wrote very fast, his head bent low as if he did not see well enough except from a close range. He did not even look at Mr. Fatumbi's lawyer. Dr. Titi Toko just stood waiting for an opportunity to speak. The judge did not give her any opportunity to address the court.

"This case is thrown out for lack of merit. The accuser is troubled; he is out of his mind. Since he cannot show up in court and he has no attorney, his case is hereby dismissed. The counter-suit is also dismissed. Mr. Fatumbi, you owe nobody any money for your wife's book business. Also nobody owes you money for your wife's death from natural causes," the judge read from his big book.

"Order!" shouted the court police.

Mr. Fatumbi felt disappointed that he was not awarded any money. He was more disappointed that his attorney, whom he had borrowed money to pay up-front, was not given any chance to argue his case before the court. Dr. Toko had bowed and said "On Your Honour," and disappeared as soon as the case was dismissed.

Dede and Furu went to console Mr. Fatumbi and his children who had accompanied him to court.

"In fact, I saw Mr. Akin this morning as we came to court. He was picking pieces of paper from the street's dumping ground. I think he is really insane. It is a pity, but I have also suffered," he told Dede.

Both Dede and Furu nodded in agreement. He might not have been involved in the book project, but losing his wife was a big blow to him. He was all of a sudden saddled with family responsibilities that he used to be relieved of for the most part by his late wife. Dede and Mr. Fatumbi did not have much else to talk about and so they said goodbye and parted.

12

Franka insisted that she would not change her name from Franka Daro to her maiden name. Who still remembered her maiden name, Franka Udi? she asked herself. Even those she attended school with now living in Lagos called her Mrs. Daro. In her workplace everybody knew her as Mrs. Daro and she signed Franka Daro to get her pay from the bank. She could not just function as a normal human being without that surname. In the past year a commission, set up to weed out ghost teachers from the many Command Secondary Schools, had gone round for a physical self-identification of the teachers. Though they had already separated and formally divorced and also carried much bitterness against each other, she stepped forward, when her turn came, to still proclaim her name as "Mrs. Franka Daro." She had no other identification. If Dede wanted her to begin all afresh in this area, he was mistaken, she told herself.

She had felt it was normal for divorcees to keep their marriage names from the many women she knew who bore the names of their former husbands. She knew a divorcee who conceived for another partner while still known by the name of the former husband. There was nothing wrong in maintaining the identity by which was known. This was her feeling until her first male friend after the divorce asked her why she continued to use her former husband's name if she was truly divorced from the man.

Brought up by a Baptist pastor uncle, Ode was not a regular church-going Christian anymore, but he still carried his childhood teachings. He felt a deep sense of unease sleeping with Mrs. Daro, another person's wife, at least as far as her name identified her. She might deny that she was anybody's wife, but he could not understand

63

why she still wanted to be called Mrs. Daro. If you had such a bitter quarrel with your former husband that led to a divorce, as she had told him, why not totally purge yourself of him, including his name? Ode had posed the question to himself rather than to her.

Ode might have kept his worries bottled up in his mind, had it not been for an unusual incident that happened one day they were alone. Franka visited him regularly. He was one of those men who did not go to a single woman's home but preferred her to always come to his. His doubts about Franka's name also contributed to this decision. Anything could happen and he could be at hers one day and a man could show up to claim her as his wife. Stranger things had happened in Lagos and he did not want to be on the front page of *The Lagos Weekend*. It was better to be careful, if one could help it, he believed.

As he held Franka, the idea that he was about to go to bed with another man's wife and commit a taboo came to his mind. He did not want to mess up his life doing what he knew to be wrong. He instantly lost his desire and became emotionally limp.

She knew that he was not sick but that something weird had taken control of him. After all, they had gone to bed many times. When he was excited, he charged like a bull. He was a man of great warmth. She felt he was caught up with a deeper problem, if she could not arouse him. As for him, he was tired of fighting a moral battle within. He wanted things to be straightened out or to have the relationship severed. He was tired of living the moral dilemma of having a single woman, Mrs. Daro, his girlfriend.

"Franka, I am troubled. Why do you still want to be called Mrs. Franka Daro after being divorced for so long?"

"Why this question at this time that we are in the bedroom?" she asked back.

"It is because we are in the bedroom that I feel like asking you," he replied.

"Don't you know what you should be doing?"

"Maybe not with Mrs. Daro," he responded.

"Is it me you want or my name?" she asked back.

"Of course, it is you I want dearly," he answered.

"Then, why does my name bother you when you can have me as much as you want? I just want to be called the name by which I have been known for these many years," she explained.

"It makes me feel awkward when I am with you and people still call you Mrs. Daro," he told her.

"That shouldn't be. Are you not a man? Can a simple name be the excuse why you are not ready today?"

He let go of her and stepped backwards. They stared at each other, each feeling that they had not known the other well enough.

Ode took one of the orange drinks sitting on a drink-stool by the bed. He gulped it, as if he was in a hurry. Franka did not drink hers. He held her hand and led her out of the bedroom into the sitting room. They both realized that their emotions had been soured and would have to wait till some other time to rekindle their desire for each other.

Franka was ready to fight to keep Daro as part of her full name, even if it meant losing a few men. She knew that many men would not be bothered by it. After all, many of them chased married women anyway and secretly dated them. It was every married woman's secret not to tell her husband the many advances made to her outside, unless such advances became really crude and unwanted. She felt that her not wearing a ring was enough indication that she was not married. She had misplaced her wedding ring even before she left Dede's house and she did not bother to look for it. After all, at no time in the marriage did Dede wear a ring to show that he was married to her. He had dismissed wearing a ring as living in the prison house of marriage.

She felt she was ready to go to court again with Dede for this part of him that she was not ready to give up. Daro was as much hers as his, she assured herself.   She enjoyed thinking about this victory and revenge. Whomever Dede married again could be another Mrs. Daro. Let him be called a polygamist. That was his problem, not hers. She was the original Mrs. Daro and would remain so for as long as she wanted.

Ode was himself divorced. At thirty-eight, he knew he had to marry again. He liked Franka but felt he had to study her. She was a very attractive woman. Besides, she was very homely. She was the sort of woman he believed would make a perfect wife. However, he did not want to rush into a second marriage as he did the first time only to break up within a few years. He did not want to be counted among people who had divorced more than once. He knew that a man who had divorced several times was suspected of having a bad character, the same as a woman who had also been divorced at the same rate. One who already had a cold from one divorce could get pneumonia from a second one, he reflected. An architect, Ode Rube supervised new houses being built by the government in Abuja, the future capital. General Ogiso was planning to move the nation's capital from coastal Lagos to inland Abuja for state security reasons. Lagos was exposed not only to a land attack but also to sea and air attacks. That was too much a risk to take for a security-conscious junta. The selection of Abuja went the way General Ogiso wanted, even though he set up a national committee that spent hundreds of millions of naira from the nation's oil wealth to

65

come to that decision. He handpicked academics and professionals who deliberated with his kind of mind and he felt good with the recommendations that he quickly accepted and decreed into law. The frenzy to build a new national capital in the savannah with the proceeds of oil sale began. Ode Rube was one of the defenders of military rule and got a huge contract for that.

Ode had been invited to Mrs. Fatumbi's book launching but did not go because he did not want to be in the same hall with Dede Daro. Who could tell whether the journalist was still interested in his former wife or not? Some men could be mean, and he was not ready to expose himself to any danger because of a woman. More so, he told himself, he had not known Franka long enough to stick out his neck for her sake. His stay-at-home attitude saved him from the unnecessary attention of being accompanied by Franka, who insisted on public appearances with him. He could not understand why she kept on reminding him about the date of the book launching. She had appeared more interested in Mrs. Fatumbi as a person than in her book. Her unusual interest in attending a function at which her former husband would be the master of ceremony to launch the respected married woman author's work intrigued him, and he stood his ground firmly not to go.

He had donated quite a hefty sum at the First Lady's book launching in which government contractors wanted to outbid each other to draw the president's attention to their generosity. Architect Rube, as he was called on social occasions, made sure he got back what he gave to the First Lady. He was not bothered by reports that strong winds had blown down some of the houses he was building for the government. He had collected his pay "up-front" and he cared not what scale of storms ravished the savannah. He had placed a bid to build houses on rocks and in the open grassland and won, and he had met the specifications of the contract.

Ode took Franka to parties and introduced her to drinking expensive wines. They attended nightclubs that were denied her as a married woman with two children. She felt happy and wanted to do whatever she could with the exception of a name change to be his lifelong partner. Neither asked the other the specific reasons for their earlier divorces. They were aware that the previous divorces would be no reason why they should not fare well as partners. Marriage, both believed, was a matter of luck.

But he also had some other plans. He was inscrutable in many ways. Franka attributed this trait to the many army officers he fraternized with. You never could read their minds. They could in one moment be laughing with you, and in the next minute be detailed to kill their very best friends.

Six months into their relationship, close to when there should be a decision on whether to marry or not, Ode became very reserved. He went out without inviting her. Later she heard the gossip that he was dating a much younger lady, Joke, a graduate of drama from the University of Lagos.

She then promised herself that she would not be bitter again about any man disappointing her. Men did what they liked, what pleased them. She would go out and seek her own desires in her own way. But now she felt she had wasted her emotions for six months, after she had almost abandoned every other thing in her life for the love of Ode Rube, who did not take her as seriously as she took him. His parting words hurt her sorely.

"If you so love me, why do you remain Mrs. Daro? Go back to him, since you are using me to while away your time before he is ready to take you back," he had told her.

"You scum!" she shouted at him.

But he was not moved by her rage and that itself told her much about the man. She no longer wanted a man who did not love her for what she was. She was surprised at the speed with which love could change to hate. But she had to assert herself.

"I will be what I want to be," she told him slowly.

She slammed the door and walked away angrily into what she feared most—dealing with a situation in which she had to start all over again. It was a humid dusk and she wiped perspiration off her forehead. The few stars that had come out barely made a sparkle. It was a waning moon and darkness must be endured until very late.

13

Things moved very fast for Dede and Furu, faster than any of them had anticipated in their chance meeting at the Iddo Motor Park. Neither of them could be complete alone anymore and each needed the other more and more. What was first suggested in the exchange of letters was finalized when they met.

"I hope you won't mind if we live together," he told her.

"How?" she asked, unsure of the nature of the arrangement that he wanted.

"I mean that we should live in one house and see how things go," he further explained.

She was not in a rush to get married. In fact, as she thought about it, marriage was not her problem. Whatever relationship that she entered into and had the possibility of her conceiving was acceptable to her. She loved him and hoped living together would bind them into a loving couple.

"Won't you give me time to think about it?" she asked.

"If you want to think about it further, you can," he told her.

In that moment days, weeks, and even months passed in her mind. It was a trajectory in which her doubts were settled. She needed no more time to decide what to do next.

"I think we can," she said, embracing him.

They remained in that embrace for several minutes, swathing one another with the other's body.

"Thank you," he told her.

"Thank you too," she replied.

Their decision to live together meant some compromise. She conceded that she would be the one to move to his place. It was not just because tradition expected the woman to go to the man and they had to comply. His job at *The African Patriot* meant that he had to be in Lagos. She was a teacher and her Grade II Teachers' Certificate was nationally recognized and so she could teach in any elementary school in Lagos. She was thus more mobile and chose to start a new life with him. In Lagos there were many private and state schools and with time she would be employed in one of them. She gave three months' notice of her quitting the job to the headmaster for onward transmission to the local education authorities. She had not covered enough years for retirement and might not have the eight years she had put into teaching counted towards her retirement, if she failed to get a government job. She felt it was a sacrifice she had to make to live with him.

They set a weekend when he would come to meet her in Warri to help her pack. They rented a pickup van that took everything she wanted to keep. He, with her beside him, drove behind the furniture-moving van back to Lagos. Her belongings were kept in a covered corner of the compound that evening until the following day when they would carefully put things in their proper places in the flat. They hoped to move to a bigger place whenever it was convenient. He really wanted to move out of the flat he had shared with Franka. He did not want his new relationship to be tainted by bad memories of his previous marriage; hence he would not mind moving to a bigger flat. He believed that some types of sacrifice were worth making, no matter the costs, to achieve certain objectives.

With Furu in Lagos, they knew that their new lives had really begun.

Soon the publisher of *The African Patriot* suggested one evening, at a brainstorming meeting of the senior staff and the editorial board, the need to review the progress in African states in their post-military eras. *The African Patriot* was always ahead of other papers in its vision and creativity, and the staff wanted to maintain that lead. This review of African states ruled by civilians was a subtle way of mounting pressure on President Ogiso and his gun-brandishing kind of rulers in Africa.

So much had been written on the military presidents and their uniformed officers without shaking them out of power. Power had gone into the heads of these dictators, who issued decrees upon decrees after suspending their nations' constitutions. It had not sunk into their heads that they were an aberration.

The civilian leaders needed to make news; in fact, they needed to be in the news more than the military. However imperfect the democratic process, these civilian leaders came to power through the ballot box and not by way of the gun. Subjects of the dictators might see what they missed by having a military dictatorship instead of a democracy. If a frontal assault did not work, another strategy had to be tried to topple the dictators. A side and sneak assault might spring positive surprises, the paper's publisher, Ena Tobore, reasoned.

A University of Leeds doctor of letters, Tobore had always been involved with the press all his adult life. He was the editor of several papers in the golden age of the press in the country. Many older people looked back with nostalgia to the days of Ena Tobore as a regular columnist when the press stood up for the interests of the people. How things had changed! There were now so many bad eggs in the press, with many accepting large brown envelopes stuffed with money from military leaders for positive coverage of a tyrannical regime. In any case, all the papers Ena Tobore once edited and wrote for had either folded up or been proscribed by the military; hence he founded a new outfit, *The African Patriot.*

Tobore named the countries he wanted covered by his senior writers: Benin, Ethiopia, Ghana, and Uganda. He would like these correspondents to spend some weeks in those countries and through observation, interviews, and research submit a three-part series on each country.

Tobore had never hidden his distaste for army boys running governments. He continued to remind the military junta that the army was established to defend the country from foreign aggression and not meant to meddle in politics. He emphasized that wherever they had intervened in politics, the consequences had always been disastrous. He could only see tyranny, rape, stealing, and torture with impunity in military governments. The litany of the sins of a military junta condemned its head to hell, he had once written. The Federal Military Government had branded *The African Patriot* the most hostile paper in the land but its publisher was not intimidated.

Dede was asked to cover Ghana. He wanted to be as close as possible to Furu, but this was an opportunity that any journalist rarely had and he accepted it. She had no reservations about his plan to leave the following morning and travel by car or bus through Benin and Togo to Accra.

"You don't need to explain further. I am happy that you are given this important assignment," she told him.

"If it were not for a journalist's type of touch-and-go assignment, I would have liked you to come along," he said.

"No excuses, dear. Journalists don't travel on duty with their friends or spouses, and I have to prepare to start teaching soon," she assured him.

She had just got an offer from a private school and had to start work in a week. She was particularly happy about the school that had a reputation for disciplined and neat boys and girls.

"It would have been an informal honeymoon for us," he said, laughing.

"We'll have a lifetime honeymoon when you return," she told him, also laughing.

"Two weeks is a very long time. I hope I can bear to stay that long without you," he said.

"Don't be too spoilt. You seem to forget that we were alone in our respective homes before we met. Go, but always think of us together," she told him.

"I certainly will," he assured her.

They embraced quietly, remaining in each other's arms for minutes. Their hearts beat as one and radiated warmth that kept them glued together.

"I think you should put together the things you'll need in Ghana. We have to go to bed soon so that you don't travel already tired," she said, as she broke from the embrace.

He had come home from his office at eleven-thirty, quite late. He had no regular closing time, but usually got home at seven on days that were not too busy.

"Don't worry; we journalists can take off within a quarter of an hour to anywhere. I'll travel light."

"Don't forget your SONY short wave radio, your other love," she teased him.

"I won't forget that. It is already in my bag with my many pens and note-pads," he replied.

"You are ready then," she concluded.

"Except with you," he told her, then held her again to himself and led her to the bedroom.

Dede Daro's three-part report was titled "Ghana: A Model African State."

In Accra you feel in your heart that you are really in the Africa we inherited from our ancestors. What do you do to the gift of a proud inheritance? You improve on its value and make it to be more cherished than before it was handed to you; you more than double its value under your care. You prepare others that you will hand over the gift to, sure that they are very ready for the next lap of the everlasting race. You invoke the ancestors and tell them that you have not failed their trust in giving you such a dear thing. For your blessing, you pay back the benevolent ones with sacrifice. That's what Ghana is today. The assignment I set out for transformed me into a pilgrim visiting a Pan-African shrine.

As soon as you arrived at Aflao, on the Ghana side of the border, you inhaled the fresh air of freedom. You said goodbye to the suffocating atmosphere before it in Togo and in our country; you moved from crude arrogance of brute power to the humility of service, from brazen corruption of the gun to a disciplined mentality of modesty, from a mind-boggling state to an eye-opening wonderland. You arrived in a model African State with a history of connections, development, and pride. You moved from ancient Ghana to modern Ghana, from the Osagyefo to JJ. The heritage of gold remains glorious.

The atmosphere there is liberating and inspiring. The icons inspire; unlike elsewhere where the paraphernalia of rulership are the gun and the koboko leather thong. See the Osagyefo's sculpted life-size figure pointing to the future confidently—there is a bright future ahead. Can this be said of other African states that appear to be stuck with the culture of warfare? See W.E.B. Dubois's resting place and your mind expands into continents of kinship. The Motherland and the far-flung family in the Diaspora coexist here. Wreaths of salvation-seekers from the entire black world deck the tomb. I shivered signing my name among those who go to give blackness a pride of humanity. I saw Stevie Wonder's wreath and signature. So were Walter Rodney's and Maya Angelou's. And many more from distant places. See Legon University, see Achimota College, and you have a feeling of African possibilities and proud heritage. They have remained citadels of learning and have been able to successfully combat decay that has taken over the institutions of brigand states.

I wept in two places, at Elmina and Cape Coast Castles, where our brothers and sisters were kept before being shipped away as slaves into foreign lands. I went through the tunnel, the gate-of-no-return, and at Cape Castle knelt at the stone shrine at which the captives poured their tears and prayers before they were helplessly taken away. After the chilling experience at Elmina and Cape Coast Castles, why should Africans not unite against the new slavery? After hearing the wails still loud in memory after three hundred years of slaves in the dungeon awaiting the unknown through the Atlantic, why should we not be invigorated by the free air of Abibiman to harness our resources? Why should the tears and perspiration of forebears not remind us of our duty to never allow ourselves to be enslaved again? Why should the torture of our brethren in those dungeons not give us the fortitude to eliminate the torture states that warrior lords have founded?

*Have we any monuments to remind us of the bad days? None!
Badagry, Koko, Ughoton, and Jeddo went through the same plight, but
nothing remains to remind the captive country's people of their woeful
past. What a difference! We forget too soon in our country and that is a
major problem responsible for our current plight. We should not forget
bad experiences in order not to make the same mistakes that led to
them in the first place. We must always remember the bad as well as the
good days. Military dictatorship is modern enslavement. In the last
years of the twentieth century some upstarts in uniform keep their
fellow Africans as slaves. What an aberration!*

*In Ghana, there is unity, quite unlike the ethnic fragmentation
and tensions deliberately promoted with bribes in jungle states created
by brigand forces. In Accra I was taken to be an Ashanti; in Kumasi I
was addressed as a Ga brother. I was no stranger anywhere in the heart
of the black people's land. I was one of the people—nothing excluded
me from the society. Everywhere in the country was home.*

*I have seen the past shame and glory. I saw Asantehene Prempeh
humiliated by foreigners; I also saw warrior Yaa Asantewa who led
troops to fight against the invaders that took her man captive. Women
thrust their arms into the air and do not rely on their bottom power.*

*It is not only natural resources that give pride to a country and its
people. Work does. Farming cocoa or whatever crops to be self-
sufficient does. It is not the ability to import luxuries from other
countries that makes a nation great, but the ability to be satisfied and
happy with what you can produce. It is not mere size that gives pride to
a nation—we know that if mere size so matters, impotent giants
wouldn't be legion.*

*I have gone to Ghana to feel the pulse of the new Ghana shorn of
sirens, shorn of curfews, shorn of brigand boots and guns, and decrees
that swell the head of generals. I have gone to the new Ghana and, after
a two-week examination, pronounce her healthy and a pride to us all.
Unlike the impotent giants, the tribally fragmented, backward looking
states that proliferate the continent, there is a true model African State
in Ghana.*

That preamble formed the first segment of his report. In two other
segments, Dede launched Ghana into the orbit of proud states. He saw
the country's development involving national pride, discipline, national
ethos, and a sense of direction.

Upon his return from Ghana, he narrated to Furu his extensive
tour of Ghana. He started, as expected, from Accra and fanned to Cape

Coast, Elmina, and Takoradi, along the coast, and then through the central region of Ashanti to the north. He stayed in Kumasi for four days. A chief linguist gave him a rare tour of the Asantehene's court and explained to him *sumsum*, the collective soul of the Ashanti nation. After a visit to the Ashanti National Museum, he went to the craft shop where he bought her an *akua-ba*.

Furu kept the akua-ba by her pillow in their bed. He told her what the akua-ba meant to the Ashanti women, who carried it on their backs. Ashanti women were a determined kind that willed to happen what they desired—conception and beautiful babies. This carving and a bright colourful compact-woven *kente* dress were what he brought back as gifts for her from Ghana.

Within two weeks of the series on Ghana being published, *Index on Censorship* wrote seeking permission to reprint parts in a forthcoming issue. Also Amnesty International's *Bulletin* wanted the preamble for its African section. Somehow these requests got to the ears of President Ogiso. Ena Tobore, the publisher, and Dede Daro, the writer of the articles, were taken away from the paper's offices for interrogation by the State Security Service for two days.

They were kept in detention cells without toilets and smelling of urine. The agents played loud music all night and gave them stale bread to eat. The few hours they were told to go to sleep, they had to stand by the cold wall of their cells or sit on the damp floor. This time the SSS men wanted these two men to understand the gravity of what they were doing with their writing. If they undermined the nation's good image again, they would taste what would be too bitter for them to report, the agents warned in cryptic terms.

The arrest served as a tonic to Dede's desire to further embarrass the president. The feverish antics of the establishment did not faze Tobore either and, in a publisher's note after his release, he promised to tell the truth about the condition of the black world. He reminded readers of the motto inscribed at the top of every issue of **The African Patriot**: "Conscience, Truth, and Humanity." Other papers praised the series of essays, as did the National Union of Journalists chaired by Chief Timi of **The Nigerian Spectator**.

On October 1 the president, as usual, made the Independence Day broadcast. In the broadcast which was made the night of October 1, instead of the dawn broadcast it was supposed to be, General Ogiso rambled about the state of the nation. He listed areas of progress and congratulated himself on the improvements made so far by his administration. The country was still one despite the tribulations of underdevelopment. Keeping the country one was a task he set out to accomplish and he had done it without a civil war. Even Europe that boasts of development has seen the splintering of Yugoslavia and the USSR, but, thanks to God, he has been able to keep a large multiethnic African country as one indivisible unit.

Peace, according to him, was at last reigning in the country after decades of coups and countercoups. He had put an end to coups. No ethnic group was fighting another group, after his army taught recalcitrant tribal leaders the ultimate lesson. He called on whoever contemplated starting an ethnic attack against another group to remember how he had dealt with groups in the Middle Belt and the Niger Delta. The cases of armed robbery had diminished drastically because of tough decrees he had enacted. Those who doubted his resolve should visit the Bar Beach on Saturdays and see the number of convicted robbers facing execution by firing squad. He boasted of having the toughest laws against armed robbery in the world.

He warned troublemakers to desist from undermining his efforts at forging a strong nation. He had enlarged his army to the largest in Africa and could cope with any foreign aggression if it arose. Any citizen that assisted foreign powers in their nefarious activities would be summarily executed. He said his eyes were watching those who had no love for the country and so denigrated it so as to give foreign agents the ammunition with which to further assault "us" and destroy the credibility of the black race as a force to reckon with in the world. *The African Patriot* carried the full text of the president's broadcast. Dede argued, as always, in the editorial board meeting that even the devil should be given a hearing to further taint himself. However, there was an editorial page, which pricked holes into the balloon that the president floated in the air. With a pathological title, "Chronic Remains," the paper asked what had been done with the national wealth within the past seven years or so. The OPEC had become an impregnable cartel and had raised oil prices three-fold and so the nation had benefited immensely from oil export. The paper asked for the wealth to be reflected in the lives of the people. It argued that the republic was being consumed by chronic corruption that made people live subhuman lives. The editorial asked why military tribunals, presided over by illiterate soldiers, tried civil cases. It also wanted to know the measures being taken to create jobs for the many youths leaving schools rather than creating the spectacle of executions. It was wrong for the government to make the people enjoy the orgies of execution of unemployed youths arrested from public places as armed robbers. The country, the paper insisted, was so brutalized that it was sick and dying and emergency measures had to be taken to avert its end.

Both Ena Tobore and Dede Daro expected government agents to visit either their offices or homes, but many days after the editorial there was no response from the junta. They were pleasantly surprised, but at the same time afraid of the president's next move.

14

Furu had started teaching at Alafia Day School before Dede returned from Ghana. She could see from her first workday the difference between the school in Warri and this new one. The proprietor-principal was a retired principal of Queen's College, Yaba, and she brought her two decades of experience of running a Federal Government school to the private school. The school had both elementary and secondary levels for parents who wanted a good education for their children and could afford to send them there. Alafia Day School did not suffer from the frequent strikes that rendered government-owned schools closed most of the year. The children were of the different ethnic groups that formed the Lagos population. Teaching history in elementary classes V and VI and civics only in class V, Furu enjoyed a rather light load compared to the six daily classes she used to teach in Warri. The pay too was very good, compared to what she used to earn.

She and Dede waited for an opportune time for them to visit Egbo and get the blessing of her mother. He was always busy, and she had to wait for a holiday period for both of them to travel. Soon they had the opportunity for a weekend trip and they set out on a Friday morning.

He drove his Datsun car. He had all the car documents that he needed to avoid police harassment. He believed in doing the right thing, rather than bribing the police. With your papers correct, the policemen at their checkpoints could still delay you but were bound to release you on your journey even if you refused to submit to their extortion. With the age of his car, the police were not likely to pay attention to him and so would allow him to pass without any problems, unlike drivers of commercial vehicles and newly imported cars.

Furu was a lively companion throughout the trip. She was naturally cheerful, but also this time she wanted to keep him awake and alert. They stopped to rest at Ofusu and decided to go to the same place where they had eaten before.

"This is our first anniversary," he told her.

"Yes, a fast one. I can't believe we were here just over a year ago," she mused.

"That's how time goes; if it doesn't fly, it slips through the fingers," he said.

"It certainly has done both," she told him.

They came out and locked the car doors. It was the breezy, cold, and dusty harmattan season. They were dressed in layers of clothes and so were not bothered by the cold wind. The sun was shining but the harmattan haze blunted its usual sharp rays.

"Do you want fish or something else for a change?" she asked Dede.

"Whatever you like to eat should also do for me. I'm very hungry," he replied.

"That means *eba* or pounded yam with the usual *banga* soup," she said.

"That's it, Furu. You know my desires more than I do, though we've been together for less than six months."

"But you gave me a clear lead. I'm not quite the reader of minds, as you will like to have me believe. But if I know what you like, that is fine. How else would you like us to be?" she asked.

"Inseparable," he told her.

He held her hand and they both strolled to their favourite spot in the line of eating sheds. They bought a big bottle of spring water and drank before the food they ordered arrived. The flavour of the soup confirmed that they had made the right choice again to eat there. They ate to their satisfaction and, to show that they enjoyed the food, left a twenty-naira tip for the service.

They rested a little to make the food go down, as Furu put it. According to her, you didn't have to eat and immediately start walking, running, or getting involved in an activity. You ate and allowed the food to settle down in the stomach before any activity, and driving was one such activity. After a while they took off, on their way to see her mother and, if there was time, to see his parents and son. Egbo and Okpara were not too far apart. If they met her mother in time, they should have time to complete their assignments in one day and return to Warri where they would take a room at Palm Grove Motel.

They left Warri early for Egbo. They wanted to catch her mother at home, since they had not given advance notice of their visit. She had a cassava farm but this time was neither the weeding nor the harvesting period. They expected her to be at home or gone not far away. Neighbours would know where she was and could easily call her if needed.

Warri was easy to drive through on Saturday morning. The experience of the previous evening when they had to crawl for three hours from the outskirts of town to the motel was not repeated. They were alarmed at the rate at which the town was growing. Warri was literally swarming with people, who had come from nearby and distant towns and villages to struggle for a taste of the oil wealth. Many did not see the wealth to taste and got stuck to the city, dreaming of a day when they would land a job at Shell. That dream was so inviting that the town had become overfilled and now spilled over into Effurun, Aladja, Orhuwhorun, and other nearby towns.

As Dede drove through the roads, he could tell that the famed oil wealth was a myth because it did not show in the town. Garbage littered the streets, gutters oozed with refuse, and the stench assaulted their nostrils. The potholes were many, and accidents were rampant as motorcyclists, bicyclists, car-drivers, and pedestrians often collided in confusion. There were neither traffic lights nor traffic wardens to direct traffic.

The sun shone on Egbo, but because of the harmattan it was cool. A small town of known traders from ancient times, the market attracted people from distant places. What you could not see to buy at Egbo was not available around. Fabric merchants, foodstuff sellers, and all types of craftspeople took their wares to the market. It was a market day, they soon realized. They saw people sweeping their sheds in the market located at the beginning of the town on the Warri-Port Harcourt Road. Some traders were already taking their goods to the market, waiting for about ten o'clock before opening their sheds.

Furu's mother was at home. When the car entered the compound, she stretched her neck to see who came in. On market days, strangers often strayed from the market to ask for direction. Somehow, she got up and came out. She rushed to embrace her as soon as Furu shouted "Mama, it is me."

"You are here so early?" she asked, apparently worried.

"Yes, Mama. I am fine."

"Thank God," her mother intoned.

"This is my friend, Dede Daro," she told her mother.

"Come in, my children," and she led them into the house.

The two-bedroom house was neatly arranged with cushion chairs and a centre-table. There was an old but neat brown carpet that covered the cement floor. That morning, as was her habit, she had swept the floor.

"How did you know that today is our market day?" the mother asked her daughter.

"I didn't know before we left Lagos. We didn't even think about what today was before leaving Warri this morning. It was as we came into Egbo that we saw traders busy taking their wares to the market that I knew it was a market-day," she explained.

"Why should you not know when I will be in? You are Egbo-born and market-days don't change and the knowledge is in your blood," she told her.

"I believe that," Furu consented.

"You have come on a good day. Your relationship will be strong and lasting," she told the two.

"We want it so," Dede answered.

"You have come early and so will need to eat, but let me get you something to drink first. What does he take?" she asked her daughter.

"It is too early to drink now, but being a market-day you can get palm wine. He likes palm wine," she said.

"It will take some time, but there is plenty of palm wine in town today. I will send Comfort to buy a gourd of it," she said.

She called Comfort, her junior sister's last-born living with her. She came in, greeted the visitors, and took money from her aunt to go to buy palm wine.

"Buy from Sodje. His palm wine is undiluted with water or sugar. Don't go to Obodo who has his gourd half-filled with water before pouring in the real palm wine," she advised.

"I know, Mama. I will go to Sodje," Comfort said, and set out for the adjoining street.

Before Comfort returned with the palm wine, Furu's mother had washed two kola nuts, which she put in a plate. As soon as her niece returned, she placed one twenty-naira note beside the kola nuts and offered them with the palm wine to welcome her visitors.

"You are my children, and one's children living in a distant place are one's cherished visitors. I am happy you came this morning and have met me at home. Dede, I have not seen you before today, but Furu told me about you after she visited you in Lagos and before she went to join you there. You are both very welcome to my small house. Have the kola nuts, palm wine, and the twenty naira as signs of my happiness that you found time to come from Lagos to see an old woman," she told them.

Dede was impressed by her cheerfulness and felt Furu had no doubt inherited that trait from her. He accepted what they were offered with gratitude. Furu's mother asked him to break the kola nut. He did, put the lobes back in the bowl, and handed it back to her. She held the bowl up to the sky. Her eyes fixed on some invisible figure up in the sky, she prayed for her daughter and new son, Dede. She asked Osonobrughwe, the Supreme God, to give them good health, long life, prosperity, and their other needs. Though her daughter had told her that they were friends, she did not want to pre-empt them should they want to marry. She felt, without saying it, that children should be part of their needs.

As they ate the kola nuts and drank, they heard sounds of gunshots. Dede and Furu looked perplexed but the older woman was unperturbed. She walked to the door and looked out. She went into the street and came back a few minutes later to meet the anxious partners.

"They have come again, the robbers," she told her visitors.

"Who are they?" Furu asked.

"They say they were dressed like soldiers and drove in a jeep," she told them.

Soon a neighbour came in to give details of the raid in the market. The traders who were already set for the day's trade either fell face down or ran in different directions when the jeep stopped and three young men began firing into the air. The robbers packed away bales of expensive fabrics and clothes and within a few minutes had jumped back into their jeep and sped off towards Port Harcourt. The traders were happy that nobody was hurt physically or killed this time. Such robberies were common later in the day when traders had plenty of cash in hand. The robbers were changing tactics as they took away materials rather than cash this time.

After the neighbour had left, Furu told her mother that she had started teaching in Lagos. She said Dede had helped her to get the job to impress on her the closeness of their relationship. Without waiting for her mother to ask any questions, she introduced him more formally to her. Both of them were starting a new life and wanted her consent and blessing.

"I can only say that both of you match each other. Go with my blessing, go with Isaba's blessing, go with the Great Creator's blessing; it is His that matters the most," the old woman told them.

"My children," she continued, "Know that from now on you will be each other's protector and helper. Let me tell you this story."

"Go on," they both said simultaneously.

She knew that her mother was fond of telling stories but did not know what story she was going to tell this time. The elderly woman cleared her throat and began her story.

"In the beginning, Osonobrughwe, the Supreme Deity, created a man and left him this vast world with so much to enjoy. Man was very grateful for the All-knowing's kindness to him. While he was grateful every day for his life's bounties, he started to feel lonely and bored. He went to the Great Maker, knelt down before Him, and pleaded that he be given a companion. 'I'll enjoy more,' he said, 'if I have someone I love as a companion to share my blessings and pleasures with,' he told the Almighty. The Supreme One understood his plight and, since He still had some of the clay left from the creation of the first human, created a beautiful woman and gave her to the man for a companion. With excitement, Man fell on his knees both for the kindness in listening to his request and in his appreciation of the woman's charm. He could hardly control his excitement and held the woman to himself in a long warm embrace. Then they set out for home.

On their way home, they began to exchange words. At first it was declarations of love. Each pledged to love the other forever and to always make the other one happy. Soon they started to exchange harsh words and to contradict each other about how things should be done. The woman was particularly sharp and caustic because the man would not take her views seriously. The woman's slightest protest enraged the man who lost his temper. After all, he was there before her and she ought to accept things as they were, he reasoned.

'When I was alone, I had peace; since you came into my world, I know no peace,' he told her.

The woman was bemused by his statement because she did not know how things were before she was created. She felt though that her companion should be sensitive to her feelings.

They barely cooled their tempers to sleep together. The next morning the exchange became more biting, as if each wanted to score an advantage over the other or even hurt the partner. Man found this unbearable and begged the Great Deity to take back his companion. He would prefer to live alone and in peace than to share things with a companion who was a thorn in his flesh.

'You asked for a companion and I gave you the best possible one. If you no longer want her company, it is all right with me,' He told him, and immediately took the woman away. The Supreme God has always had the power to make and unmake.

Even before Man reached home, he was burdened by silence. He could hear his own breathing and wanted dialogue with some other person, however sharp. When the wind blew, he was frightened as he thought some wild animals wanted to attack him. In addition, he remembered the ecstatic love experience of the previous night—at the most pleasurable moment they had sung meaningless songs to each other—and could not control his desire. Whom would I fall upon now that this strong desire had seized me? he asked himself. He shouted to break the stifling silence, 'O my Great God, I want my partner back, I want back my love; I want my beauty, my woman back!' Osonobrughwe told him that He had heard his appeal and brought Woman back to him.

They quarrelled again, and Man went back to Osonobrughwe to complain about his lost peace and to request that he be relieved of the cause of his headaches. He again took back Woman from his life. But Man did not wait for daybreak before going back to the Great Maker to get her back. This to-and-fro daily experience went on for six days and on the seventh, He told Man and Woman: 'Since both of you always quarrel and yet cannot live without each other, go away and find your own solutions to your problems.'

The Supreme Being, for His part, withdrew to an impossible height where He could no longer be reached by human beings. And that is why men and women have the kind of relationship they have today—they cannot live without each other and yet are always quarrelling," Mama concluded.

Both Furu and Dede clapped and laughed at the end of the story. They did not need to be told its meaning and import.

"My children, will you advise that I put my money in Bright Age?" she asked.

Bright Age was one of many investment houses in the area. When one put in money, one got back five hundred percent of the deposits in a period of only six months.

"Mama," Dede advised her, "Don't throw away your hard-earned money. It is all trickery."

"But some people are already getting back the returns of their deposits. Onoge invested one thousand naira six months ago and yesterday collected five thousand naira. I saw him dressed in new clothes at the funeral of Tekevwe, your father's relation. By the way, you have to go there to see what burial ceremonies have become. His children have spent more than a fortune," she told them.

"Mama, keep your money with you; don't put it in any investment company," Dede reiterated.

Mama had been slipping out now and then, but it soon became apparent that she was preparing food in the kitchen outside. The aroma of the food filled the air and wafted into the sitting room. She brought in the palm oil fish soup with starch and yam.

Dede could see that Furu's mother prepared this food meant for the gods and important people as a mark of approval of their relationship. They washed their hands together in one bowl and began eating, as they talked and teased each other. It was a most delicious meal prepared with the expertise of an experienced cook.

Dede and Furu did not have the time to go to Tekevwe's funeral. He wondered out loud, as they drove back to Warri, why people that feared death so much that they would not demonstrate against tyranny and would do anything to prolong their lives, even when they were miserable, would like wakes and funerals so much.

"You should have asked my mother," she told him.

"I hope she knows," he said.

"I am not sure, but there may be a story explaining it that she knows," she told him.

Early on Sunday morning, they drove to Okpara to see Uvie and Dede's parents. His parents had travelled to Kokori to watch the famous Egba Festival and were not likely to return in time. They had gone with Uvie, who was said to be inseparable from them. While he would have liked to see the cultural performances of the Egba Festival, they did not have the time to go there. He avoided the Lagos road at night. The policemen and soldiers transformed into armed robbers at night and he would not take the risk of encountering them. Besides, with the potholes and the dangerous bus drivers, a night journey had to be avoided.

They could not spend more than a few more hours before returning to Lagos that same day.

"At least you now know where I come from," Dede told Furu.

"Who told you that before now I didn't know where you come from?" she asked him.

"But if I had been a spotless man, as in folk tales, what would you have done?" he asked back.

"But did I meet you in a market?" she retorted.

"Iddo Motor Park is worse than a market," he teased her.

"But you are not spotless like those spirits or frogs that transform into handsome men. I have known a bit of you now to say that," she laughed.

"If I were such a deceptive ogre, it would have been too late for you to realize that and escape," he told her.

"But what if I was one of those spirit women that lure men to bed and kill them?" she asked.

"Then it would have been too late for me too!" he laughed.

The visit to the Delta was quick, as they had to be back in Lagos that Sunday night. She had to go to work as he too. She felt fortunate to have that job and wanted to put in her best.

15

Until she met Chief Ugbo, Franka did not realize she could be in another relationship or in love again. Did her people not say that an animal that had escaped from a trap avoided an arched stick, perhaps another trap? Was the same caution not exercised by a fish that had once struggled out of a hook in avoiding whatever metal-held bait it came across? She had felt strong and so believed that the winds of love would no longer blow her into its tender directions. But she would discover before long that reason alone was not enough to ward off temptations. And temptations could be many and very strong.

Chief Isaiah Ugbo was in his early forties, a stocky and cleanly shaven man. Already balding, he joked to Franka about his permanent shave on the forehead. Somehow, she felt the early baldness gave him an air of responsibility; he was more elderly, more mature-looking than the men she had known. He had risen to the position of Chief Manager at the National Brewing and Bottling Company and earned quite a fortune. In addition, he had a lot of authority in the distribution of the company's drinks. With weddings, burials, conferment of chieftaincy titles, and other parties a permanent part of the nation's life, having enough drinks was always a major concern of the people. Knowing Chief Ugbo gave you access to beer, malt, and soft drinks that made the people happy and, upon all, bought at a reasonable company price.

His house was impressive from outside. Painted white, the big duplex building perched on a hillock in the Ikeja Government Reservation Area of Lagos. It had red aluminium roofing, which distinguished it among the imposing houses in the area. The house had a high fence around it, and a heavy black iron gate added further protection against any intruder.

He was a very important man despite his relative youth. A

gardener, who also acted as a day watchman, took care of his compound. The lawn was mowed regularly. One had to be rich to live in this exclusive area, and Chief Ugbo was very rich. The five-bedroom house was lavishly furnished with state-of-the-art chairs and decorations. He had a taste for art and had acquired some of the best paintings of the nation's renowned visual artists, Bruce Onobrakpeya and Dele Jegede. Once inside, you knew that the outside was not deceptive but really reflected the inside.

Chief Ugbo drove a Peugeot 505, which many felt he did so as not to be seen as too rich. Two of those who worked directly under him in the company each drove a high-class Mercedes Benz. The chief could afford a Mercedes 500 if he wanted. Many people who knew him felt he feared for his life, and his habit of modesty warded off armed robbers and other evil-minded and jealous people from doing him harm. Outside, he did not draw unnecessary attention to himself. He lived a peaceful and quiet life and mixed with very few people.

Four years earlier, he had, as soon as he had woken from a dream of having an educated wife, asked Agnes, his wife of ten years, whether she was interested in going back to school. She had married him after her secondary school. She had to put on hold her desire to go to the university because of the marriage. Many of her friends who were anxious to marry encouraged her to marry first and get her education later. They persuaded her to believe that a woman soon gets over-ripe for marriage, but not for education, some of which she already had in secondary school anyway.

Agnes herself had always secretly envied female graduates who held their heads high on public occasions. They spoke fluently, they attracted attention; they were chosen leaders. There must be something in a university education, which gave confidence to women who were graduates. She enthusiastically accepted the offer and within six months was registered in the Mass Communication Department of the University of Lagos. Her husband had taken care of what was necessary for her admission. She did not ask him how, because it was common knowledge that knowing people in high positions was the key that opened the gates to the university. To ask Chief Ugbo how her admission was processed would mean questioning whether he had influence in Lagos's social and economic circles. Of all people, she knew her husband had clout. He chose to operate quietly but he achieved whatever he set out to do.

In her final two semesters, Agnes and Chief Ugbo agreed that things would be more convenient for her if she lived in the student hostel rather than go through the daily grind of the notorious Lagos traffic. That traffic sapped the energy even from the most energetic. It doused the brains with smog and one never thought correctly for hours after going through it. It turned many of its victims into physical wrecks. She had heard her professor of urban geography in one of her elective courses describe Lagos traffic as a crucible, and she did not want to go through the crucible every day in a crucial period of her studies. She had classes as early as eight in the morning from Monday to Friday. This semester she was spared Saturday classes. Chief Ugbo came to take her home on Friday evenings and brought her back on Sunday nights.

Franka surprised herself again that she could be attracted to another man soon after breaking up with Ode Rube. She was more surprised about herself since she knew that Chief Ugbo was married. Many years back, when she was younger, she would not have contemplated having an affair with a married man. She would have condemned it as a fruitless relationship. However, she was now a different person. Going to any length, as she learned from the divorce case, was not always pleasant. She had felt a void in her life, which she found hard to bear. She needed that void to be filled and, in pursuit of that, she was ready for the bitter and the sweet. She believed she had gone beyond the worst. After Dede and Ode, what relationship could be worse? She questioned herself in an attempt to assure herself of a better future. She wanted a serious man, married or unmarried, rather than an irresponsible single man of her age or younger.

Chief Ugbo cleared the dark clouds of her fears from the beginning, and that made her to trust him all the more.

"I'm married, but we can still be very good and close friends," he told her.

"Where is your wife?" she asked, holding her breath.

She was expecting so many possibilities. His wife had gone home to deliver a baby. His wife was away to cool down after a misunderstanding. He had left her in their hometown or village far away to be visiting her there once in a while. Many men in Lagos did not trust their wives enough in that flirtatious city and so kept them back in their less sophisticated hometowns.

"At school," he told her.

"Tell me about her," she pressed him.

"She is a student at the University of Lagos, where she is studying Mass Communication. She stays in the student hostel from Sunday night to Friday evening," he explained.

"Why do you trust your wife with so many young students and

lecturers? Have you not heard of their love stories?" she asked, as if concerned for him.

"I have never thought of my Agnes as the type of woman who would misbehave."

"Is she not human?" she asked.

"She is, but I trust her."

"And she trusts you too! But Chief, let me not drill you," she said, laughing.

Her laughter eased the atmosphere and made him to feel comfortable with her.

"By the way, how do you cope in her absence?" she asked.

"Somehow I do. She prepares enough food for me for the week and my cousin living with me helps a great deal."

"What of in areas other than food?" she asked.

They both burst into instant laughter.

"You must be wonderful," she told him.

She now knew how to raise men's desires and when to cool them. She was learning fast and putting into practice her little experience.

"Thank you. I really want us to be friends."

"Let me think about it," she told him.

She did not want to be taken for granted. Any relationship at all had to start at her chosen time and not his. She would sleep over it and give him an answer when she was convinced about what to do.

For a week she thought about the friendship proposal. Then she went back to him on Monday night to give her response. She wanted him. Chief Ugbo would not make her feel that she was old because she was divorced and had two children. She was still much desired by relatively young men, even if they were married like him.

The chief was at home alone. Standing by the door, she could hear Fela's music. The Afro-pop king was in his elements in "Shakara Woman" that she also liked. She gently knocked thrice on the door. He came to open the door and looked pleasantly surprised at seeing her. They shook hands, which she found a little too formal. She was not used to shaking hands with men, but once the chief had stretched his hand she had no alternative than to extend hers for a handshake. She had not informed him that she was coming to see him. However, she knew that it was time for his wife to be in the university campus and the chief would be free to welcome her.

She wore an intricately embroidered gold-coloured *buba* and headtie. Her high-heel shoes were also gold-coloured as well as her handbag. Her makeup was subtle, her fragrance an exotic blend of a pleasurable smell. She was gorgeous.

"I hope I am not disturbing you?" she asked.

"Not at all! How can you disturb me? If you like, disturb me as much as you can. I'll love it," he said.

That night Chief Ugbo promised her many things. He would register her as a distributor with the brewing and bottling company. If she wanted a loan to do contracts, he would speak to one of his bank manager friends to process her application in the shortest possible time. He could make her a rich woman.

She had come prepared to hear from him compliments, and he poured out from his soul so many things to her.

"You are extraordinary."

"You are the angel of beauty. No beauty parallels yours."

"You are more than a queen, so graceful."

"You are Cleopatra."

"You are my Miss Universe."

All she could say at the end of the litany of praises was "Thank you, my dear."

She sharpened his appetite by teasing him with her body but not giving in. She knew that she had to carry herself in a way to be highly desired. She would not be cheap to win over. She would torment the man for a night for him to desire her more and more. Chief Ugbo behaved as if he had not been married for so many years, as if she was his first date, and he felt ashamed that he could not control himself.

Her misgivings about men had not completely disappeared. She knew that giving in to him that night would be a mistake. She needed to dangle herself before him so that he would crave her even more. Men appear to value what they find difficult to get, she believed. She would play hard to get to bed with him. She undressed, kissed him, allowed him to fondle her as he pleased, but would not allow him to come into her. She had taken good care of her body, which still bristled as a woman in her prime. She behaved as if she were a virgin and not the mother of two children already.

After that week, Chief Ugbo felt he had worn down her defences, but it was all her strategy. She then threw herself completely at him. It was as if she was diving into a deep river for the pleasure of her life and she didn't care if she drowned and died. She wanted the experience. She had been careful and that had not helped her much in the past. Now she would be carefree, even careless. She did not care now about being that usurper and much-abused woman, the other woman. She dreamed and saw the two of them, Agnes and her, sharing the chief like a slaughtered bull. Both of them were scrambling for the choice parts of the chief. She could not believe the energy that drove both of them in the effort to get the most of him. She even tasted raw some of the parts she garnered into her big bowl. All she cared about now was her own self.

She was free to pass the night at the chief's and he passed some nights at hers. From very late Sunday nights to Friday mornings was a love feast from which both walked away always feeling exhausted.

Both hoped that things would remain the same or grow stronger. But another excitement suddenly entered Chief Ugbo's life. This excitement he shared with his wife, Agnes. At this time the unexpected happened. Still childless, Agnes believed that her going to the university was a magic wand that had broken a sad cycle. She became pregnant at last. If she could not be pregnant the past ten years but only in her last months in the university, God must be praised. God always works in a miraculous way, she told herself.

Chief Ugbo started to look to Friday evenings as he also looked to Sunday nights with intense excitement. He wanted to be with Agnes and he also wanted to be with Franka. Each provided him immeasurable pleasure though of a different kind. He wished the two pleasures could coalesce in order for him to have the two women, wife and lover, at the same time. The entire week was now filled with excitement for him.

The news that Agnes had conceived brought a spark to his weekend. At long last he was going to be a father. Though married for so many years, he had doubted his virility because of his wife's inability to conceive. Now what had seemed impossible had happened. Despite his wealth, he imagined other men not envying him because of not having a child. Now he would have a child of his own and see himself as a complete man. Had he not taken a mistress partly with the secret hope of her conceiving? He wanted to impregnate a woman, wife or lover, and fortunately it happened with his wife. May Jehovah be praised! he chanted silently.

The exhilaration that filled the chief's house from Friday evenings to Sunday evenings did not last long. Agnes soon felt like one waking from a happy dream and plunging into a nightmare, which made her very miserable. The cycle might have been broken but the hope did not grow into fruition.

She was entering the second trimester of the pregnancy when she started bleeding. She lost the pregnancy drop by drop of blood. The doctors at the University Teaching Hospital made every effort possible, but they were unable to stop the bleeding.

Chief Ugbo who had been excited about the prospects of having his first child was emotionally distraught. He went to his New Age

Church of Christ to report his wife's miscarriage. The prophet had been his confidant and counsellor all the years he had been in Lagos and saw him rise from supervisor to chief manager. He felt he owed his progress to the prophet's prayers. One routine he had not broken despite the passionate relationship with Franka was attending the Saturday night service with Agnes.

After spending some moments in the innermost temple, the prophet came out and told him that his wife's pregnancy had been "sucked away" by a jealous woman who wanted him for herself.

"That woman is a cobra and you must keep away from her before she hurts you even more," the prophet warned Chief Ugbo, one of the pillars of the New Age Church of Christ.

Chief Ugbo and his wife sat on the front pew, reserved for the main pillars of the church. It was after church service that many deals in the National Brewing and Bottling Company were struck. The prophet was proud that such an illustrious man was a devoted member of his congregation. He never lacked funds to complete the church's projects.

"You must cast out the demon from your life," the prophet said, waving his forefinger at the chief.

This mystified Agnes, but the chief understood the inference. Only Mrs. Franka Daro fitted this description of the veiled evil one, the jealous woman, the cobra, and the demon. He knew that she had become very comfortable with him, calling him "Dear," "Honey," "Darling," and "Sweetie" as a woman would call her husband. She was in control of the house for more days than Agnes and this might have gone into her head, he thought. Was she trying to charm him into marrying her? The prophet spoke in parables, and he had to heed his warning.

Chief Ugbo bid his time. He realized that however tenderly it behaved a cobra should be treated with caution and be rid of. He would chase this human cobra off. His wife would graduate in a few weeks, and while he had been planning for a double celebration, he would now have to prove that he had some will power. His plan was laid out and waited for execution.

On July 10, Mrs. Agnes Ugbo received her Upper Second Class Bachelor of Arts degree in Mass Communication at the convocation ceremony. The University's Visitor, His Excellency General Ogiso, President of the Federal Republic, was there in person to hand out the certificates. That evening Chief Ugbo threw a lavish party for his wife to celebrate four years of what he described as "fruitful labour."

Before it was time for the party, the chief sent his cousin with a note to Franka.

Dear Franka:

I don't know whether I should address you as 'Dear' from henceforth, but what is important is action and not mere words. I hope you know that I am in the middle of a celebration, but you may not understand well why today I should have been the happiest man on earth. But let me come to the main point, lest you miss it.

Don't come to my house again. I want to leave you in no doubt that I will not come to yours either. Consider our relationship as ended, dead, and something that cannot rise out of its sinful ashes. I want to desist from sin. My life with you has been a long sinful act that I feel so ashamed of.

I want the sacrament of holy matrimony to remain sanctified. The life of the flesh to which we succumbed ourselves the past six months was very Satanic and a sentence to eternal damnation. I pray for forgiveness that I fell to the temptations of the flesh, which I know destroyed Sodom and Gomorrah. I am now born again in the blood of Jesus. I plead in Jesus's name that you go back to where you rightly belong, to Mr. Daro. After all, you still use his name and love him despite your denial. No amount of love can take the place of a stable marital life and a happy family. For you and me, consider our relationship as ended. May the blood of Christ save our souls from the sins we committed in the name of love.

Yours in Christ,

Chief Isaiah Ugbo.

She could no longer be surprised by men's unpredictability. She had gone through this before and it was not as painful as the first time when the stab was cruellest. This was still a betrayal, but she had gained experience in bearing such a stab as this. She folded the letter and threw it into her handbag. Asked by the chief's cousin and messenger whether she had a reply, she shook her head. However, on second thought, she beckoned the boy to come back.

"Tell him that I am not surprised. I prepared for this from the very first day I knew him. Tell him only that," she told the boy and opened the door for him to get out.

She would surprise others and herself, she swore to herself. If men had to be men, she had to be a woman. The men sought their own self-interests, and she would be stupid not to find hers too.

16

Dede Daro wrote a weekly column in which he was able to express his opinion about anything he wanted. He soon became so used to writing it that it gave him no trouble at all. He also wrote an occasional special column titled "Matters of the Moment." It was this that challenged him the most. He prepared for these "matters of the moment," investigated, and read widely for these special essays, but usually he wrote them under a spell. When the muse gave him a nudge, he woke and jumped from bed to his desk to start writing in a frenzy of inspiration.

Furu had witnessed this act several times. The first time she saw him do it, she felt either something had gone wrong that he suddenly remembered and wanted to put right or it was just a weird mannerism. She saw that he went on writing for a long time until he returned to bed. Subsequent similar acts had made her used to his inspirational frenzy. He left food or her company for the summons he knew he must answer instantly, if he was not to miss a brilliant piece.

He had for several weeks been thinking of the nation's financial houses, which he knew were really racketeering institutions. They filled every town, and the entire nation was obsessed with them. Furu's mother's inquiry about them had kindled his thoughts about these scams. He went to have an extremely rare clean cut and shave. He then put on simple clothes, and set out for the special task. He did not want to be recognized as Dede Daro, the journalist; that would impede his investigation. He wanted to introduce himself, if asked during the process, as a teacher, office worker, transporter, or trader. He wanted to fit the picture of any possible trade or occupation at his age. He changed clothes the same day and on different days to better fit possible occupations. He also dressed according to the possible amount he claimed he wanted to invest. He knew what his people expected the rich and the poor to look like respectively, from flowing robes of brocade to basic cotton dresses.

Dede enjoyed and hated the new roles he was acting as an investigative writer. Switching from one occupation to another and on and on made him realize how it felt like to be in a specific socio-economic class. He did not play the role of a police officer or that of an army officer. He resisted playing the role of what he called the vulture class in the animal kingdom of his country.

And so for days he visited many of the financial houses, asking the owners questions as if he wanted to invest in them. They all painted a sunny picture of the future, and talked like master diviners, perfectly convinced of the financial returns that would transform a wretch into a wealthy person. They behaved like miracle-workers sent by God to change the face of the African earth from poverty to riches, if only men and women, young and old, had faith and invested *now*.

He also talked to the investors he met at the financial houses and in the street. He asked them what they needed to do with plenty of money. The poor wanted to be rich to be able to afford their desires; they felt they were missing so many good things in life and they counted cars, fine houses, and clothes, among their needs. The sick and the dying sought wealth as a way to ease their situation; many of them felt that with money they could have the type of treatment and care that would save their lives. Of course, the rich wanted to be richer to always be in an unassailable position in their society.

He realized that the country had a lot of problems, as everybody he interviewed wanted to be rich in cash and not in kind. He found nobody who wanted to change the direction of the country, none who wanted to ease the suffering of the miserable millions around. There was none among the people who wanted to make money in order to set up an orphanage or buy equipment for the crippled or the blind. None of the already rich that wanted to be even richer ever thought of having a foundation dedicated to solving one of the major human problems of the country. There was not even one among them who daydreamed of recruiting and arming a secret force of desperadoes to overthrow the despicable dictator despoiling the land and restore democracy.

Everybody who wanted to be rich gave a list of luxury items and gadgets that he or she would buy. And these were all imported from abroad.

Then one morning, just before he left for work, the creative spell seized him. Fortunately, he had no specific appointment that day to put him under pressure to get to work early. Like an experienced patient of a chronic disease, he knew when an attack was imminent. Responding to the call from within, he reached for his pen and notepad and started to jot down what came to his mind.

The Inverted National Pyramid

Karl Marx spoke of religion as the opiate of the people. I would say that daydreaming about wealth is the opiate of the people in this country. Every other building in Broad Street and elsewhere is a bank, investment or financial house of sorts. They have big offices in skyscrapers. You are told to invest two thousand naira in a "trust" and expect in six months that your investment would mature and you would take away ten thousand naira. This is an insane interest rate.

Our pyramid of values is upside down. Instead of building a broad base, which can carry the rest of the body, we have the opposite. The small base cannot sustain a broad and weighty top. The investment gurus take money from you to pay mature interests to earlier investors. The big robbers of the national wealth are reinvesting what they have stolen and making obscene profits. The poorer people investing give cover to the robbers. Now there is a stampede to invest and only fools and a blind government will not foresee the imminent collapse of the inverted pyramid. Already the structure in its early months tilts dangerously to one side. It is only a matter of time for it to collapse and crumble. And that is not far away.

Men are kidnapping children for money-doubling rituals to make money to invest. Housewives are hawking sex in the street to make money to invest. Parents are pandering their daughters for money to invest. Children are stealing from and killing their parents to have money to invest. Armed robbers are of many categories now, ranging from street boys and girls to university students and those in uniform. Now that army and police officers are being caught as armed robbers, we can see how far the love of the new god has gone into our heads.

We have heard of the woman who sold her husband's Peugeot car when he travelled abroad, thinking she would make more than ten times the money she put in. When the man returned earlier than expected, the secret investment became public news. They are still waiting for the investment to mature as they take taxi to work. They may have to wait their entire lifetime to realize the folly of daydreaming.

Every church service devotes more time to collecting money and offerings in cash and talking about investments than prayer and readings from the Bible. Professors, students, traders, army, and police all gather what they can get through fair and foul means and invest for tomorrow's wealth. Daydreaming about wealth is the new social leveller. The poor see themselves as in dire need of getting out of poverty's stranglehold; the rich want to sit unassailably on top of money so that they could never be poor even in their next incarnation. Everybody wants to be rich without working, just as everybody wants to go to heaven but does not like to die. We have become a captive nation, each person holding others hostage to exploit.

Ono O. Ono has more security guards than many foreign presidents. His brigade of guards is commanded by a retired general, one of those retired in his early forties. The nation's revenues are used to guard a government-sanctioned swindler. Military boys are posted to guard Ono O. Ono. He appears to be the Controller of the Federal Bank. Bales of fifty naira notes fill his many warehouses. The long trailers carrying money to and from warehouses have police escort cars blowing sirens for motorists to clear the way. If you think they have no right to do that and stay on the road, the stone-faced police would whip blood from you.

What a pity! People whose rivers have been destroyed by oil spillage forget about their farming and fishing and daydream of becoming millionaires through phony banks. Others whose farms have been made barren by gas flaring forget their plight and daydream of turning into instant millionaires. Those fishermen and women whose rivers and streams have been clogged by oil blowouts forget about their occupation and daydream of becoming millionaires.

Once hooked to the opiate, one cannot be rational. The daydream will only end with a crash into reality. Parents whose children had been shot dead for demonstrating against government neglect have turned to worshiping a new god. The agitation for oil companies and the Federal Government to do more to clean the polluted environment is gone. The angry dog has been given a sop and has lost its bark and bite and gone to sleep. University students have forgotten about their tradition of shaking society from its anomie and gone the same path of daydreaming through wild investments.

Ono O. Ono has become a god and pastors pray to him. Their congregations go on a pilgrimage to touch Ono, the non-denominational prophet of the new god. Since he has the Midas touch, wait for gold, ass-heads! What bothers me is that the government has conferred on him the respectable Order of the Federal Republic that was denied such heroes as Joseph Tarka, Aminu Kano, Tunde Idiagbon, and Ransome Kuti.

What should be the responsibility of a nation's rulers to the exploited subjects? Should a government be satisfied that it has succeeded in diverting from itself the rebellious rage of a discontented people into the pursuit of El Dorado? Should a government be happy that it has quieted social unrest without firing a shot? Why should government-sponsored programs such as book-launchings and parties for visiting foreign dignitaries be occasions for investment house proprietors to flaunt their wealth? They are even introduced as the entrepreneurs of the New World Order!

Very soon, very very soon, the inverted pyramid will collapse and the destruction will be felt nation-wide. Egypt built a real pyramid out of her total knowledge of the sciences and the arts and sweat. The Great Pyramid at Gizeh was meant as a tribute to God. The inverted pyramid of our country is a tribute to corrupt Capital, the new Mammon.

When the people wake from this daydream and find out that they are far worse than before, they would be uncontrollable. Let those who take the people for a jolly ride, beware.

Dede Daro's "matter of the moment" in *The African Patriot* caused strong ripples all over the country, especially in government circles. The cabinet debated it at a full meeting and considered arresting the errant writer and closing down his paper indefinitely. However, it considered the present time the worst of times to take such measures, and President Ogiso agreed that no action should be taken hastily. It was several days before the visit of the British Culture Minister, Lady Betty McEwen. The opportune time of the foreign visitor saved Dede Daro from being immediately accused of inciting people to riot against the Federal Military Government and maliciously discrediting the government before its hardworking citizens.

Chief Ofe, the new Information and Culture Minister, would cite Dede Daro's article in the welcoming address to Lady McEwen at the airport as an example of the liberalization and free speech that characterized the current administration's policies. Though a serving officer, Colonel Ofe chose to be called Chief Ofe after a little known traditional ruler conferred an insignificant title on him. For some reasons, General Ogiso did not mind.

Dede's critics were many. There were death threats from churches, from those claiming to speak for Ono O. Ono, and from anonymous sources. Some Pentecostal churches devoted their Friday night vigil to praying for the incarnated evil spirit called Dede Daro to be bound eternally. Word reached him that a popular pastor who relied on donations from his rich congregation went as far as characterizing him as a demon and prayed that God should destroy him. The shouts of

"Amen" in response to the pastor's prayer for Dede Daro's destruction echoed all over Lagos that Sunday morning.

When in a few weeks, the financial houses started to re-write the laws of their agreements by extending maturing time from six months to one or two years and reducing interests drastically to only twenty per cent, everybody was reminded of Dede Daro's recent article. Two months after the appearance of that "matter of the moment," Ono O. Ono fled the country and started the infectious collapse of the investment houses. It was rumoured that the Chief of Police had escorted him in disguise to fly out of the country. Dede could only smile and say "At least, I warned you."

But he was mistaken that the victims of the scam and others would praise him for his foresight in forecasting the collapse of the investment houses, which started to collapse, at first month by month, then week by week, and soon almost day by day. Block by block the pyramid was unravelling. As the news of the collapse spread, others began to close down in a panic. The directors fled to parts of the country in which they were not known, to avoid being lynched by crowds of disappointed investors. The richer directors fled overseas through the porous borders of the country.

The public was dumbfounded and felt made a fool of by a group of articulate crooks. Many people, who saw a bleak life ahead of them without getting their money back, died of suicide, heart attack, or stroke. Many others became afflicted with hypertension. A few sank into irrecoverable depression, just as others became mad from the shock happening. The collapse of the investment houses destroyed more lives than any epidemic had done in the country's history. Armchair and ivory tower statisticians wrote that more people died from the financial earthquake than from cholera, polio, and smallpox combined in their deadliest years.

Strangely enough, the fooled populace could not get at the proprietors of these financial houses. Those who were literate and had read Dede Daro's article turned their anger on him. His name became a household topic. At Ajegunle, a woman called Didi barely survived when her car was set ablaze because somebody shouted her name. Some said she was the one who destroyed their lifetime's investments. It was useless that she was a woman and not a man that Dede was, since the shame of being fooled had destroyed the people's senses and thus made them to lose their vision.

Furu's colleagues at school read and discussed Dede's articles. Many of them in the school had invested in the financial houses and lost their money. Parents of the children had also made investments and lost. When some of the parents knew that she was the devil's wife, they thought of calling a Teacher-Parent Association meeting to ask the principal to relieve her of her teaching position. Her husband had ruined them, they complained. Fortunately, the principal argued against it and they calmed down.

At school her colleagues advised her to restrain her husband lest he put himself in unnecessary trouble. They cited precedents of government critics who had been jailed or liquidated.

"Who can save this country?" they asked her.

They had given up on the nation's many problems.

"Perhaps, only God if He took pity on us and did not continue punishing us," one of the teachers said.

Furu knew how passionate Dede felt about the issues and advising him to stop writing would be futile. If she could not stop him from writing, she might at least stir him to be more general in his criticism of the national malaise.

"Some day they will understand the good you are doing and you will be vindicated," she told him.

She was afraid for him, but she felt helpless.

Ena Tobore was as blamed as Dede for the omen that brought the collapse of the investment houses. The sale of his paper went down for days. Those who used to buy the paper felt too stupid not to have listened to the warning and directed their anger at the messenger. Even vendors, who had spent their meagre savings on the investment craze, did not muster enough courage to sell the paper for several days.

Ena Tobore, a visionary but practical man, suggested sending Dede out to Addis Ababa as the paper's Chief Foreign Correspondent, but he refused to leave under pressure. He would rather wait and see the public and Government later realize their mistakes than give the impression that he should be sacrificed for the bad news that could have been avoided.

The victims of the investment scam regained their senses gradually and for the first time a letter to the editor praised the paper for its foresight and courage. Similar letters followed, praising the newspaper for its vision. *The African Patriot* soon surged to overtake other dailies in sales.

17

After Man and Woman had been together for many months, according to the later part of the myth of creation, the woman woke up one morning after a blazing full-moonlit night to see her belly bigger than normal. At first she was as perplexed and petrified as her naive companion about the cause of this swelling. Maybe she was eating too much, they reasoned, and she decided to eat half her usual portion. She even took an herbal purgative to pass away any excess in her stomach. She had a running stomach for several days. But as more weeks went by, the stomach got bigger and bigger despite her near starvation and purgation. She suspected she was sick from a strange disease. She was certainly weaker than her normal vivacious self. It was worse in the morning when sometimes she felt like vomiting. Her appetite grew sharper still. None of the herbs they knew could cure her of the strange ailment.

It was months later when she felt some unusual movement inside her stomach, as if a small animal was cavorting there, that she became so scared she was about to die, she cried to Osonobrughwe for help. She confessed to the Almighty the sins she felt she might have committed that could be responsible for her plight. *When my man wanted me, I told him that I was sick when I was not. I am not happy that I do almost all the house work when he sits waiting for me to fulfil his desires. I don't like his shouting at me. He never seeks my advice before doing anything on behalf of both of us. Sometimes I tell him that I love him when I don't. I hate him when he says that I am complaining too much and leaves me alone to suffer pain.* The confession did not reduce her growing belly. Short of what to do to cure herself and afraid of dying from this strange affliction, she cried, "O Osonobrughwe, help me out of this!" The Supreme One, though far away, heard her and, since they were not squabbling and disturbing Him with complaints anymore, decided to put her fears to rest.

He told her that the affairs of night would come to light by day. The potbelly that she was developing was the exhibit of their continuous lovemaking. He, the Supreme Creator, would no longer make more human beings. Man and Woman, the first two humans, would remain his original patent. The two people He created would henceforth generate more human beings by acts of love. They were the first father and mother and their offspring would fill the earth. It was then that the two understood that the woman was big with a child. The Almighty One impressed on them that their offspring would consume their attention, and that could increase or reduce their usual squabbles depending upon the manner they handled their affairs.

Furu, who had wished for a child almost twelve years of marriage, least expected a break in her unproductive cycle so soon. The first few days after her period was due, she felt the cycle had started its wild game again. It had been irregular many times over the years. Even when she was alone without a man, it happened; but she knew that hers was not going to be one of those mysterious conceptions that she had heard about. She was scared though of conceiving when the faceless man was visiting her in her dreams. Sometimes her period came as late as a week or more after her anticipated date. Now she felt a little bloated and yet hungrier than usual; she felt weaker and yet more excited and restless when she woke in the morning. Soon she knew that there was a great change coming to her life. Within a few more weeks, she had all the signs flashing all over her body. She was very sure of her new state before telling Dede the happy news.

His instant response was to embrace and congratulate her. He laid his palm on her umbilical cord area and smoothed the stomach gently.

"The akua-ba has done its work," he teased her.

"Did you know that for the past three months I have been carrying it on my back once in a while?" she asked him.

"I didn't know, but it has worked fine," he told her.

"I am so happy," she said.

"Of course, me too," he replied.

The weeks and months following her pregnancy brought a new atmosphere to the house. She was excited and expectant. She could not yet believe that she was pregnant. She tried to do the things she used to do at a fast pace, but Dede advised her to be careful.

"I hope you know you are climbing a nine-month mountain and

should be careful," he told her.

"Of course, I know that. But carrying a child is not a disease that should disable me," she answered.

"Just be relaxed," he advised.

He felt if it were possible for a man and a woman to carry the pregnancy together, he would have borne his part heartily. This was not the time for him to be away all day as he used to be, chasing stories and experiences that would inform his columns. He had to do his work as well as help at home.

"Don't forget to carry the akua-ba on your back," he jokingly admonished her.

"I didn't know you are a medicine man. I won't forget, if carrying it on my back will give me a beautiful child," she told him.

"Why do you say that, as if you are expecting a girl?" he asked her.

"Not at all, I am fine with whoever it is. A beautiful boy or girl is all I want," she assured him.

"I was afraid that you might have a gender preference. You know that there are more women than men already in the country," he teased again.

"I know where you are going," she said.

"Where am I going?" he asked.

"Where many men will go," she said. "You want to say because there are more women than men already we should give birth to more males to narrow the gender gap."

"I was joking. Give me any child and I'll love it," he told her, as he drew her to himself.

He helped in the house chores. He did the dishes after meals and fixed some meals for both of them. Usually, he did the blending of tomatoes, okra, melon, and onion. She was the chef who put the magic taste to the pot with her touch. Once the soup or stew was done, he prepared the *eba* or boiled the rice and beans to accompany it. On some occasions, the two struggled to do the same things.

"I appreciate your assistance," she told him.

"It is always a pleasure," he answered.

"How many times do I have to tell you that pregnancy is not a disease? I can do the things that I used to do," she told him.

"And some things better, I know," he said.

"I don't know about that!" she responded.

They both laughed. Her complexion brightened and glowed. She was happy, he was happy and they showed it in their cheerful mood.

They started to prepare more seriously for the baby's arrival after the sixth month. Both agreed not to check about the sex of the expected baby. They bought a cot and other items in the maternity list. As for the clothes, they followed what had become the tradition of buying a girl's clothes that could be worn by either a boy or a girl, whichever was born.

When the time came, Furu understood what it really meant to be in labour. It was more excruciating than any pain she had known all her life. Not even the pain of whitlow that afflicted her right thumb and kept her sleepless at night would compare to this pain. Nothing you were told earlier prepared you for it. You had to go through it to know it firsthand. It was torture when the pains started to come at shorter intervals. But she bore the pain of labour with dignity and wept tears of joy after the baby came out crying. To her, this had taken long in coming.

Dede had followed Furu to the maternity ward. At the crucial time, he was told to stay behind when the nurses took her to the delivery room. While the nurses were very composed, he could feel his heart beat fast and awkwardly. At some stage he felt it was better to feel the labour pain itself than the emotional pain that nobody else observed. In the meantime, he practiced the breathing lessons he had learned from his yoga and mystical readings. He took deep breaths and exhaled. He found a space in the waiting room where he took first the cobra position, then the eagle, to slowly inhale and exhale. Then he took a very deep breath and exhaled with a long drawn-out *ooommmm*. He focused on just his body, following from the head through the neck to the chest, stomach, and legs. He started to pace up and down the hallway. He really felt lighter at heart. He thought of more exercises to do to while away the time.

Within minutes, one of the midwives who had asked him to stay in the waiting room came to inform him that his wife was stronger than he was. He did not have a chance to ask why before the midwife proclaimed, "You are the father of a bouncing baby girl."

18

Those who knew her were surprised that Franka Daro had enrolled to study law at the University of Lagos. She abandoned her teaching job to be a full-time student. She did not go for the part-time or weekend program, either of which would have made her keep her job and still take a degree however long it might take. She wanted to put her heart, body, and soul in what she did, hence her drastic move. She had always liked having a good education. After her National Certificate of Education, if she had the means, she would have continued straight to have a university degree in education. But she was practical to stop there and work and marry and settle down. Suddenly she realized that she needed to study more; she wanted to have a university degree. But she had changed her mind on what degree to pursue; she was no longer interested in teaching. *Teaching is not going to lead me to where I want to be. Teaching has not changed my life. I don't want to manage all my life. I want to be a very important woman by all means. I want to live a high life. . . .*

The law degree took a long time to complete. You had to put in four to five years of study, and that depended on whether you had the national certificate of education or the school certificate before entry into the university. On graduation, you had to go to the Law School for a year in order to be called to the Bar. You had one year of national service after all of that, and you still had to serve an apprenticeship of several years before you were free to set up your own chambers. It was a time-consuming and tough profession, but she felt that if she put all her resources together, she would be able to obtain the degree without too much trouble. She had always liked having a good education and now was happy that she would have more of it.

For personal reasons, law excited her. Deep inside her, the divorce and custody cases made her to see law as a profession in which she would always know and exercise her rights despite the truncation of legal procedures by the military.

Yes, at her age and with her experience, she did not need to work too hard to get what she wanted. This is her country and, as long as you know the right strings to pull, you can get anything you want, she reminded herself. Everything is a game and once you master the rules, you will be in a position to win through either skill or loopholes. She knew her assets and she would employ them to get what she was hungry for. To be called Barrister Franka Daro was something that would give her the highest satisfaction. With the degree, she would append LL.B. to her name. That would bring much respect. A degree in law would also lift her from poverty to a wealthy position, if she organized herself well after graduation.

She knew from the beginning that she was not going to practice law. Many of those lawyers were pitiable. Always saying "On your honour, sir" without making a point. She was not ready to depend on begging clients to get cases. She wanted a more dignified way of living very well; in fact, she wanted to live very big. She felt that several years in the university would change her into a very expensive commodity. She wanted the degree; she wanted to be a graduate of the University of Lagos, from where Architect Rube's girlfriend and Chief Ugbo's wife had graduated. She wanted to be as capable as any woman. And the degree would make her very capable. That would open many doors for her in a country where doors open or close automatically depending upon your association or the company you keep.

Franka raised seduction and bribery in the university to an advanced craft. She had conducted oral research, checking from older students and graduates how things went on campus and was able to gather information about what to do to ensure a smooth passage through the corridors of academia. From the very first week, she bought expensive gifts for her lecturers. She gave very fine dresses to them and their wives. She then enticed her younger male student colleagues, who were happy talking with her, into believing that she would sleep with them sometime in the future, if they were patient enough. Somehow, her male student helpers knew that she was too sophisticated for them, but they hoped and continued hoping that, as they helped her do her assignments, she would surrender to them. By the end of the first semester, she scored As in all her five courses. And this was accomplished without the least amount of effort.

Her female student colleagues also played the game, but were not as adept at it as she was. She told herself that she could not afford not to get good grades and she wanted to be doubly sure of that. She did not want to give cause to anybody to laugh at her, and that informed her actions. She did not want to fail in whatever she now did. The marriage fiasco was now behind her, so were the relationships with Architect Rube and Chief Ugbo. *I will not embark on anything again and fail. I will not fail again. I must use any means available to me to succeed.*

Some weeks her class attendance was irregular. She took time off on weekdays to visit friends. She found time to attend more parties than ever before. Being introduced as a student of law at the University of Lagos made her more conscious of her worth. So on campus she had lecturer and student boyfriends. Outside she had high-society friends. She started with the commandant of the Command Secondary School she had resigned from, a lieutenant colonel, who was soon displaced by a full colonel who left when a brigadier came in. Publicly the brigadier was her friend, but she had many secret lovers whom she introduced as her relatives or former colleagues.

Brigadier Eugene Otu was one of those senior officers of high status but with a non-strategic appointment. He was neither a divisional commander nor a corps commander. He was also not in the Armed Forces Ruling Council. He had his office in Army Headquarters and all junior officers saluted him all over the place. He had enlisted in the army after secondary school during the civil war as a second lieutenant. He fought in the same front as the President who was then a lieutenant and, fortunately, they were always two major towns behind the frontline that saw brutal fighting.

The brigadier valued his closeness to the president and could reach him in the office without the hassle that other senior officers went through. After all, at the rear of the civil war front, both General Ogiso and he had daily picked from the same pool of favoured refugee women to sleep with. As if to reflect the spirit of national reconciliation, he had, also like the president, married a refugee wife. He had only one wife, unlike the president with many wives tucked in the presidential mansion. His wife though had been sickly and he kept her even as he flirted.

Now he headed a task force on rehabilitation of educational buildings. It was a deliberately vague portfolio committed to nothing. The government budgeted to the office millions of naira that he did not have to account for how and what he spent. He knew in the generous spirit of the junta that General Ogiso expected him to do nothing and he did nothing. In fact, nobody outside his small office had heard of this task force, one of so many to keep senior officers happy and occupied with how to spend free millions of naira rather than be restless and be planning coups.

Brigadier Otu, in one of his rare visits to schools, had seen Franka at the Command Secondary School when she was still married. He had learnt of her divorce from the school's commandant who did not disclose that he had briefly dated her before a colonel took over. Once the brigadier showed interest, the colonel withdrew.

The brigadier paid Franka a monthly allowance of fifty thousand naira, far more than the combined monthly salaries of three of her lecturers with large families to cater for. She knew that army officers who were loyal to General Ogiso sat on top of money and could take away as much as they wanted. She had earlier seen that from the Command Secondary School, where most of the teachers were army officers' wives. They came to work in expensive new cars, while she took a taxi to work. She saw the money that Brigadier Otu was giving to her as part of the circulating process of capitalism as practised under military rule in the country.

It was while in the latter part of her first year in the university that she told her brigadier friend that she needed his help.

"You know that whatever you want, I will always do for you," he told her.

"Don't say that. I could be Herod's daughter and you will be finished!"

"You aren't that wicked!"

"How can you tell that I cannot be wicked if I choose?"

"Okay, what do you want that you think I can do for you?" he asked.

"It is big and small, but very important to me," she said rather quietly.

"I order you to tell me," he told her in a mock military tone.

"My mother needs a house. Since my father died, she has been managing to live in the old and dilapidated house, but she needs a house of her own. Our custom expects me to build one for her," she told him with a coquettish smile.

"That is big but small to me. I will take care of that. Let's work out the details later."

She was elated and embraced him, then gave him a kiss, a privilege she kept from her many friends.

"Thank you. You have made me great," she told him.

"It's my pleasure," he responded. "You are dear to me and it is my responsibility to do whatever I can to make you happy."

"You are wonderful," she complimented him.

Within six months the house was built, a big modern edifice in Arhagba. Her mother could not believe it at first, but it soon dawned on her that her daughter had made her rise from rags to riches. How many women of her age and widowed had such a modern house? She relished her dream world. Motherhood was really great, she realized.

The Okpe king sent for Franka to be given a chieftaincy title, a call she respectfully answered. She was given the newly created title of the *Anama of Okpe*. She was very smart and her people at home recognized this and honoured her for it. How many undergraduate ladies built fine houses for their mothers? She was the first in the kingdom.

The brigadier accompanied her to the installation ceremony. He came with many officers, whose clothes cost more than the annual salaries of most civil service workers. It was the best of such ceremonies since Eseze II came to the throne. The Okpe monarch loudly praised Okpe women who were so influential that they could bring brigadier friends and high government officials to pay homage to him in his humble palace. He used the occasion to tell the brigadier that he was qualified to be a first class traditional ruler and the chairman of the state council of chiefs and that he should whisper this into the ears of the state governor, his subordinate. In response, Brigadier Otu praised Franka Daro as a well-brought-up lady who was a source of pride to him. He promised to do everything possible to make the Okpe king what he wished for himself.

Close to the end of her first year in the university, she found herself in the same hall with her former husband. Dede Daro had become very popular in the universities for his weekly and occasional "matters of the moment" columns. The law students' union invited him to talk to them on "The military, rule of law, and human rights." The Main Auditorium was the venue. Though the lecture was open to all, the lecturers kept away for fear of losing their jobs. The Governing Council of the University had in the past three years dismissed twenty lecturers for what it described as "political impropriety in an academic institution." The lecturers and administrative workers therefore avoided any gatherings and lectures that appeared or could be seen as hostile to the military regime. They knew there must be spies in the campus gathering to report to the military government what transpired at the lecture.

The auditorium was, however, filled with students. Franka sat in front so as to be seen by Dede, who should have already heard that she was a law student, she guessed. He should know that as he had gained popularity, which he had always pursued, so had she elevated herself career-wise, as a law student. She was not doing badly, and she was not one of those divorcees that their former husbands would laugh at for retrogressing. *After the lecture, if students go and shake hands with him, I will go so that he will see me close. I look fresher than when his wife. Let him see how I am a beauty queen again.*

Dede walked in and gave a low bow as greeting to her. He had, since the divorce, felt that the animosity was unnecessary, more so as they had children together. After the student union president introduced him in glowing terms, he stepped forward to go to the podium to deliver his speech. There was an air of anxiety as to what he was going to say, with many in the audience expecting him to lambaste the military on their record in governance, as far as law and human rights were concerned.

It happened so fast in the huge hall that many did not grasp what was happening till a moment later. Three grim-faced men stepped forward and did not find it necessary to introduce themselves as secret service agents on orders of the government to stop the lecture. They preceded Dede to the podium to declare that the lecture could not take place.

Once the students realized what was happening, pandemonium broke out. They shouted "No!" in unison, and started throwing pieces of paper and other missiles at the three men. When one of them drew out a rifle and fired through the window into the air, everybody ran for dear life. It was later that Franka learned that the law students' union president had taken Dede to his room in the hostel that night for his safety.

Dede's article on the subject that he was prevented from addressing in the university campus appeared three days later in *The African Patriot.* Students cut out the piece and pasted copies of it on walls and boards all over the campus. Nobody on campus could ignore reading the banned lecture. Military rule by its very nature was hostile to the rule of law and democracy, he wrote. Ruling by decrees was most undemocratic, and worse still if ruled by what he described as an "illiterate soldiery." He called military rule an "aberration and an affront" to humanity and civilization.

Franka read the article and knew that Dede had not climbed down from his high ideological ground. He was still the defender of the underprivileged, the champion of the poor and oppressed. In fact, he had become even more critical of the government. He seemed to enjoy taking high risks, which the people applauded. He continued increasing the level of endangering his life. That was a risky business with such a military junta as General Ogiso's. She knew from her friendship with Brigadier Otu how dangerous it was to toy with the president, one of whose praise-names was the Leopard.

To her, Brigadier Eugene Otu's friendship ensured her survival. She was a realist. Let Dede continue being a dreamer, or rather a daydreamer.

19

Tetebe, water lily, was the name that Dede had prepared for the expected child if it turned out to be a girl, which it did. Furu lost out in the naming bet, because she had prepared a male name since she expected a boy. Tetebe was truly a water lily, fair and beautiful. Both parents competed to take care of her. If the mother breast-fed her, the father fed her from the plastic feeding bottle. If a baby had two mouths, Tetebe would have been busy sucking, drinking, or eating from both at the same time. Dede washed the used napkins. After he got the warm water ready, he called on Furu to give the baby a bath. Tetebe made Osonobrughwe's intention of having children to be fulfilled. She really consumed much of their attention, binding the couple into one loving family.

The baby looked well-fed and healthy like those babies used in advertising expensive baby foods on television. Her skin was silky and it glowed. Everything about her was superb. She gave pride to her mother when she went to the clinic and other mothers complimented her child. They even asked her for the type of baby oil that she used in rubbing her and the food she fed her on. Many teased her that her baby would be their son's wife when grown up. She laughed and told them, "We'll see what happens when the time comes."

By the second year, the girl started to have frequent fevers, which made her parents take her to the hospital for a check-up. Her blood test confirmed a family problem that Dede had forgotten about and least expected would resurface in his child.

It was the girl's swollen hand that first led him to remember his lost brothers and sisters. Then the yellow eyes, a sign of jaundice, confirmed his fears. He pored into the eyes, used his two hands to open them, and saw the yellow at the root of the pupil. The part of the eye that should be blood-toned was whitish. He knew from this that his child was anaemic. Then came the pains and his worst fears were instinctively confirmed before the hospital re-confirmed the two-year-old baby's affliction.

The paediatrician at LUTH, Dr. Lateef Laoye, assured Furu and Dede that the sickle cell disease had passed its fearful phase in the country.

"Times were," he said "that diagnosing sickle cell disease was like passing an immediate death sentence. Then sicklers didn't live beyond five years. That was the age of *abiku*, days of superstition and ignorance, rather than this enlightened age of modern medicine. Later, their average life span climbed to the age of ten, and then sixteen. Now, with good hospital and home care, many can live close to normal lives. I have read in a recent issue of *The New England Journal of Medicine* that in the United States, the average life span for men with sickle cell disease is 48 and for women 52. And many have lived up to sixty years. How many so-called normal people in this part of the world live beyond fifty anyway? As long as there are no serious complications, there should be no fear for the sickler's life. Pray and be hopeful. Your daughter has a good chance of living close to a normal life. Take this booklet, *A Parents' Handbook for Sickle Cell Disease*, and read it carefully. Your daughter can grow up healthy in spite of the disease and become whatever she wants to be."

"Thank you, Dr. Laoye," both parents said in unison, heaving a sigh of relief, now that they realized they were in no immediate danger of losing their daughter to the vicious disease.

"Bring her for a check-up every three months, unless there is an emergency. Some of the kids I used to treat are now my students, who are becoming doctors and researching into every aspect of the disease. Our forefathers must have known some roots, herbs, and barks of trees to deal with this case. One of our proverbs states: 'For every sickness there is a cure in the forest.' Already there is one of our doctors in Texas, who is trying a drug made from indigenous herbs. There are other doctors in the United States who are testing a drug that can be used to enhance haemoglobin f so that the sickling process can be averted. Every child has haemoglobin f, also called foetal haemoglobin; hence sicklers do not show signs of sickling the first nine to twelve months of their lives. After about a year they lose the haemoglobin f and start to show signs of sickling. The new drug tries to interfere with the genes to restore the haemoglobin f. We'll live to see a cure for the sickle cell disease."

"Amen," Furu and Dede intoned.

Tetebe progressively got well, and soon she became her normal restless self again. She tried to turn things upside down as if to test their durability and in the process she broke many things. She ran in the house as if it were an open field and often bumped herself against the wall. Many times she frightened her parents with her hyperactivity.

Furu took the advice of Dr. Laoye to breast-feed the baby till she was two years or till she wanted something else to eat. She followed instructions in the *Handbook*: giving her a lot of fluids, not allowing her to play in the hot sun, not exposing her to cold or wet things, and taking a tablet of folic acid daily. She added a tablet of multivitamin a day on the advice of friends. If this was the price she had to pay for her child's health, she was more than ready to do so.

20

Dede made sure that he created the time to attend the first meeting of the National Association of the Disabled (NAD) to which he had been invited as a special guest. He could recollect, clearly, his discussion on the disabled with Mrs. Fatumbi when he visited her at school to check on how far she had gone with preparations for the book launching. She had told him about the effort she had to make to build a ramp into the classroom for three of her disabled students. It took more than six months to convince the school's principal, the self-styled provost, to agree to do it. With the assistance of students, the construction cost only two thousand naira. Once it was done, the students wheeled themselves into the classroom, and she noticed that their grades improved considerably and she could only guess their improvement was a result of the self-worth they gained in taking themselves into the classroom.

He had often thought about the neglect of the disabled in the country and how they were not properly cared for. But respecting the memory of that sensitive woman was a compelling reason for him to pursue the issue.

At first he thought he had missed his way to the venue of the meeting. He then looked at his invitation card and saw it was the right place. After all, he had come to this place several times, including the infamous occasion, almost a year ago, when his lecture was proscribed by the secret service the very moment it was supposed to start. The atmosphere was like that of a Pentecostal revival, crowded and noisy. The disabled, their friends, and relatives had all come. Many civil war veterans, who were without any disability, came to register their solidarity with their unfortunate brothers and sisters.

Outside the hall, Dede watched hefty men carry in leg-less men and women. Many of these amputees had been victims of land mines that both sides of the civil war had used to their strategic advantage. They did not have the financial resources to buy wheelchairs. Mothers strapped big children on their backs. Many club-footed adults hopped about energetically. Some leaned on their canes, but others just hopped and rested after a while. The blind were there, led by relatives. The deaf stood among the throng, gesturing with hands and head in answer to signs.

Many students and campus workers were curious and thronged the hall in an effort to see so many disabled people together, and the crowd waited to see what would transpire there. People came from all over the country, north, east, and west, and spent much to be at the formation and inaugural meeting of the National Association of the Disabled.

When he was nominated without opposition to be the president of the NAD, Dede felt ambushed and caught, but he did not want to fight his way out of the nomination. It dawned on him immediately that someone else other than the very physically disabled themselves could effectively preside over the affairs of the association.

He was called to the front and asked to address the new association. He walked through the noise and took his place behind the big table. There was silence of anticipation. What was the journalist going to say about the many disabled of this country? Then he began to speak.

"Ladies and gentlemen, I accept, with a high sense of responsibility, the office you have given me," he said, and was interrupted by a prolonged applause. There were howls, cheers, and clapping of hands in appreciation of his acceptance of their choice of him as president.

"Order!" shouted a huge man with a clubfoot in the front row. And then there was silence, as they waited to hear more from their president.

"We are all disabled in one way or the other," he continued. "Mind you, some forms of disability may not be visible. In nature there is the law of compensation and all humans succumb to it. Everybody has a disability, which may not be visible. Others outside this hall are as disabled as we are, regardless of their appearance of wholeness. Of course, we are all born equal and should be treated equally."

"Sure, sure," the clubfooted man shouted.

"This association has much to achieve in making the public and the government aware of the plight of the disabled in our society. They are treated as if they are a reject caste that people should be ashamed of. Do you remember the time the Sudanese president visited?"

"Yes," they chorused.

"What happened?" he asked.

There was a noisy answer, which was barely comprehensible. Then he pointed to one woman who had tried to shout above others.

"They cleared the streets of crippled people as if they were dirt," she said in a voice filled with anger. "And that was because the president of a country where there is enslavement of many of its citizens was visiting us!" she added.

"Yes, the government was ashamed of its own citizens and forced them from every main street that the visiting president would pass. We should be ashamed of our leaders," he said.

"They deserve to be thrown out," the clubfooted man shouted.

"Yes, let us not talk about the government for now, but every human being deserves to be well treated," he told them.

He saw rage on many faces because of constant humiliation and used his hands to gesture for calm. Then he went on.

"Let me tell you my personal experience of a few disabled people. In my youth there was a cripple at Ughelli who was the best-known basket weaver in the whole Niger Delta area. Up till now there has been no basket weaver like Okpeku. Also, a blind masseur at Kiagbodo attracted patients from all over the South and his hands worked miracles on ailing men and women. Yenrin restored health to many people and particularly brought health to married women to conceive. And all over the country, you have heard of Malam Dogo, the solo singer, whose songs have been played by local and foreign radio stations. His voice is divine. Malam Dogo is here with us," he said, as he pointed at the blind minstrel from Ilorin.

Malam Dogo, a man with an impressive stature, stood up and was applauded. He waved his right hand, bowed in appreciation of the recognition, and sat down.

Dede resumed his speech.

"Here in Lagos, Brother Sango, though crippled, controls traffic when the police and traffic wardens abandon their posts to take pepper soup and eat specially prepared goat's head with the money they have extorted from motorists. We know that under Brother Sango's charge, Lagos never has a better flow of traffic. I understand he is unable to make it today, but his wife is here. Let's give her a round of applause for having such a patriotic and industrious husband," he told them.

They rose and yelled "Brother Sango!" for up to three minutes and the self-appointed marshal shouted his "Order!" so that Dede could complete his speech.

"The disabled have rights and demand to be treated as humans. Every public building like this hall needs to be wheelchair-accessible. This change should start with our schools. We have many disabled children who cannot go to school because the schools are not built with their needs in mind. Government, industries, and corporations should implement this improvement immediately. Look at the scene today before we started this meeting. Big men and women in wheelchairs were lifted up the high steps. Many don't even have wheelchairs. This is an affront to their dignity. The disabled are tired of being humiliated. Government should subsidize the purchase of wheelchairs, walkers, braillewriters, and other types of equipment used by the disabled to survive. The blind need specially trained dogs to go anywhere they want. Let these be this association's share of the national cake!"

"Yes, we want our share," somebody thundered from behind.

"Government should build schools to train sign-makers to help the hearing impaired. Above all, there should be training programs for different categories of disabled people. By this, I mean vocation schools. From human experience, one form of disability tends to sharpen a hidden talent. The disabled deserve to work as other human beings," he said in a high voice.

"Yes, we demand equal treatment," shouted the clubfooted marshal.

"Ladies and gentlemen, you have shown more courage than any group in this country. Keep on with your determination. You give me the boldness to speak out even more loudly than I normally do in order to serve you. By the way the disabled are treated the entire world sees for itself the type of people we are in this country. We will start working on a plan of action to give you your rights and make your life more comfortable. We will start by having a national register of the disabled. From this register support groups will be organized to assist every disabled person. The struggle you have started today continues. We shall overcome our disabilities. Thank you."

Everybody, who could, stood up and clapped and howled. A chant passed from lip to lip, "We shall overcome our disabilities!" The chant was taken up by others outside and spread all over Lagos. The crowd milled out of the hall in excitement.

Later, Dede learned, the Army Headquarters was put on red alert until it was discovered that it was the newly formed National Association of the Disabled that was chanting its slogan. The government did not care about its people chanting, singing, and dancing. Once worn out, they would go home and fall into deep sleep that gave the government plenty of respite. What they did in their dreams posed no threat to the military junta.

The African Patriot reprinted Dede Daro's speech. The paper also wrote an editorial calling on the government and people of conscience to make life more comfortable for the disabled. The country was wealthy enough to provide basic needs for the disabled, it also said. The editorial called for a national awareness week for the disabled to sensitize the public to the plight of the disabled in the country. While the family should be the core of the support group, the government must play its role also.

Dede knew he had impressed an important point into the national conscience and hoped for a new beginning for the disabled nationwide.

21

Franka made a major decision at the beginning of her second year in the university. She had a lot of stock taking and reflection to do during the long vacation. She came back to school with renewed vigour and new ideas. She was confident that she would always be able to find her way through academic difficulties, but the law profession was too time-consuming, she suddenly realized. After graduation, there was another full year at the Law School, where only a third of the candidates passed and then was admitted to the Bar. The law profession took such a long time to complete, and she did not have the same patience as the other law students much younger than her. If she could plant her seeds and see them grow to fruition in one day, she would prefer that. She had just purchased a microwave at one of the superstores on Allen Avenue. Microwaves accelerated cooking. If she could microwave her education, she would. The earlier it was completed, the better; she told herself.

How would she practice in court after bribing her way through the university and the Law School? Then the wind would blow feathers off the fowl's behind and everybody would see the eyesore! Franka did not want to be like one of those "On-your-honour-sir" attorneys, who begged to represent clients for a pittance. Many waited in courts or police stations to solicit those who were arrested to bail them out for pay. Apart from the likes of Titi Toko, Mudiaga Odje, Mitaire Unurhoro, and Richard Atijegbe, most other lawyers took taxis to court because they could not afford to own a personal car. Maybe she could sway judges to rule in her clients' favour. In their first year in the law department, the future lady attorneys already discussed such contingencies of influencing judges by any means necessary. But she could not depend on that all the time because some judges were as unmovable as a rock. Others were as unpredictable as the coastal weather. It was this realization that made her decide to take a different course.

Looking for a shortcut, Franka reasoned that a degree was a degree. After all, apart from academics, who cared what field people graduated in? All that was important towards realizing her goal of making money and living comfortably was a degree. She decided to change her major to English.

Fortunately, she had taken three core English courses in her first year. Yes, she took the boring Advanced English Composition (ENG. 201), as well as Introduction to African Literature and A Survey of English Literature. The Faculty of Law required that all its students, irrespective of year of entry into the program, must take equivalent compulsory courses in English. To be skilled communicators to argue cases, they must have a firm grasp of language and human experience that English provides, it reasoned.

Though a student, Franka carried that maturity of comportment and an irresistible charm that made university administrators listen to her. She was able to exploit loopholes in the English Department's requirements to meet her needs. Since she entered with her national certificate of education, an advanced level equivalent, and had taken the compulsory 200-level courses, she was accepted as a third year student. Fortunately for her too, the grade point average was calculated from the 300 and 400-level courses. So, thanks to her secret deals and gifts, she won a major academic victory.

For the next two years, she took courses that were very practical and capable of enhancing her personality as an educated woman. She knew she was not going to work with the English degree, but she wanted her spoken English to be outstanding. She took the phonetics and speech courses taught by Dr. John Osgood, an Englishman, so that she could speak more fluently with a "been-to" accent.

She was becoming a good English speaker, thanks to university education. Those gadgets in the language laboratory made you feel like a disc jockey, but they did a very good job as you imitated the English native accent. She created free time to go to the language laboratory to learn outside class periods. Though she gave out gifts profusely to assure herself of an A or a B grade in every course, she put her head and heart into those courses that she felt were necessary for her future. That future was full of possibilities.

Five years after her divorce, three years at the university, she graduated with a BA Upper Second in English. Brigadier Otu, who had been too busy with office work to notice her flirtations at school, suddenly became even closer to her.

An Okpe lady chief with a degree in English and a "top military brass" as her boyfriend was worth more than ten untitled and unattached women graduates combined. Her convocation party really proved that she was more than so many other female graduates put together. The party drew many VIPs from the nooks and crannies of Lagos, ranging from corporations and parastatals, to the armed forces. President Ogiso heard about the party and donated the entire kitchen and bar, both inexhaustible.

Guests drank local beer and imported wines. State caterers prepared an array of traditional and foreign dishes. Some of the guests had not tasted those exotic dishes before and ate as if they were holding hunger at bay for another week or more. Some of the ladies stuffed their handbags with fried meat and chicken kebab to take home to show as evidence of the lavish nature of the party. They danced to highlife, juju music, as well as to Congolese soukous and reggae.

Well into the middle of the party, Brigadier Otu signalled the disc jockey to stop playing music. He clapped thrice to draw attention. Dressed in an overflowing brocade robe, he was in a very jovial mood. Everybody waited for him to speak.

"Ladies and gentlemen, I have a special message to read," he announced.

He then read the president's congratulatory message to Franka Udi:

My government and people are proud of your diligence and industry and celebrate with you a hard-won degree. Felicitations!

Everybody stood up and gave Franka a standing ovation. The smiling celebrant curtsied from one direction to another. She felt proud about her success.

As the night went on, and with the influence of different wines, the dancing became dirtier and dirtier. The ladies flaunted their buttocks at the men. Many half-exposed their big breasts in the spirit of a party of this sort. Partners held tight.

Many contacts were made and love deals struck that night. Franka had brought in only unmarried female graduates and students, who dressed deliberately to tease the sexual appetites of the men. The ladies were like hunters who wanted to end up with a big kill and most of them succeeded. Little did the men know when they thought they were chasing the ladies that they were themselves going to be netted into experienced women's bosoms! That night launched Franka into the career of a wealthy dealer.

She was supposed to do a mandatory one-year national service after graduation, but she ignored her posting to Borno State.

"What will I do in that desert—ride camels? I hate those ugly animals. Better spend my time riding Baby Benz in Lagos," she told one of her fellow graduates who had been posted to Benue State.

"You know Benue women are very good at handling men. Have you seen them dance? Any man would desire them. Do you want to compete with them? What, other than huge yams, will you get in Makurdi or Gboko?" Franka asked her.

"That's why I have come to you for help in re-posting," she pleaded.

With Nkechi, she started what was to become a constant assignment, the fixing of ladies with top army men and, in doing so, penetrating the army hierarchy to its very top.

Brigadier Otu treated her to a two-week vacation in London.

"With your degree in English, it is only fair that you visit England. You'll have to tell people that you've been there," he told her.

That had been one of her dreams and she was overjoyed by the vacation gift. They flew first-class to London. In the plane she realized there were many luxuries she had not experienced before then. The air hostesses pampered them throughout the long flight. She watched movies, drank expensive wines, and ate the best dishes available. General Otu had done for her what no other man had ever done before. She had arrived at the top class of society, she believed.

She was impressed by what she saw in London: the planned streets, the many bridges, the walks by the River Thames, the sense of order, the constant light, and the cleanliness of a huge city. But she was not a town planner come to study how an old city worked.

She spent most of her time outside the hotel in Marks & Spencer, Oxford Street, and Liverpool Street's Flea Market. She did not see anything interesting in Trafalgar Square that tourists talked so much about. The huge statues did not impress her. What were pigeons to her? She would not mind if they all died of hunger or some disease, she mused. Nor did she find the trip to the grounds of Buckingham Palace or various parks, including Hyde Park, exciting. It was all crowds. She felt she did not leave Lagos to come and see crowds in London. She felt she had seen enough crowded streets at home. Let all these tourists take photographs of people and places, but she would be a photograph herself to the people.

They visited Madame Tussaud's Wax Museum and she adored Cleopatra. She would like to carry the charming poise of the Egyptian Queen that brought emperors to her court. She stared at her for a long time and, before leaving, gave a military salute she had seen officers give to Brigadier Otu to the beauty of all ages that she saw in Queen Cleopatra.

To her, the whole trip was a shopping spree. After all, Brigadier Otu had called the trip a treat and she wanted to be fully treated. Knowing that her friend had unlimited resources, she picked items with both hands, threw them into the cart, and caused a stir in shops. The salesladies at Marks & Spencer looked at both of them and smiled mischievously, as if wondering what she was going to do with all those dresses and shoes. Another Imelda Marcos in the making or what, they must be wondering.

The brigadier did not only pay for the purchases with large sterling bills, but rolled the cart after her like her personal bodyguard. She was a queen of a foreign land come to England to shop for the latest fashions around. Out of the shops, Brigadier Otu carried the shopping bags until he waved down a taxi to take them to their hotel in Kensington. Back in the hotel, she reciprocated by treating the brigadier to different styles of lovemaking they had watched on late-night cable television.

Later at Heathrow, her four oversize luggage items went unchecked into Eagle Airways destined for Lagos. The airline officials had, in fact, run to Brigadier Otu and her to take the luggage pieces from them and checked in everything without weighing them, unlike other passengers' items. She smiled to herself and now saw why everybody sought power. Power sweet-o-o, she secretly murmured. *Power makes you important. Power makes you free. With power there is no suffering. I want to have power that I can exercise all the time. Power gives you what you desire.* She saw the many uses of power that make people seek it by whatever means possible.

Brigadier Otu paraded her as "My English graduate girlfriend." Franka had foreseen what a degree could do for her—it would raise her to an enviable level. She was now a high society woman, beholden to one brigadier and yet beholden to no man. She made it known to him, whom she now called Gene, that though they were friends, she owned herself. She was mature enough, she told him, to take care of herself and did not want any man to stalk her or pry about where she went.

It did not take her long to decide what she wanted to do as a graduate. She received a letter of exemption from the National Youth Service Corps without applying for it; thanks to Brigadier Otu's telephone call to the Director of the National Youth Service Corps, Colonel Edem. In the Armed Forces, a junior officer never refused a senior officer a favour as simple as this.

She saw the trade in art works as a logical step in her career. Many companies and institutions needed art works to decorate their offices and grounds, and she would commission artists to make works or buy completed works to sell. Many of the artists were almost starving and whatever she would buy from them could fetch her quite a fortune. She was going to be a collector, a dealer, an agent, and a promoter of art all in one. She would also register as a contractor with both the Federal and Lagos State Governments. Being a contractor was part of the road to success in the country. Government officials infatuated with her would give her a windfall contract, which she did not need to execute to receive a fat check. She easily registered as a contractor to operate all over the country. Again, thanks to Brigadier Otu who made the necessary phone calls.

She rented a place on Broad Street, a large-spaced floor out of which she created a small section as her office. She furnished the hall with bright-coloured art works, *adire* and *kente* fabrics, and glossy posters from American sex-addicted magazines. She saw nothing wrong in placing a replica of a Benin queen headpiece beside a mini-skirted skinny American blonde. That was art, whatever would draw people to her shop, she imagined.

The shop was large and had display glasses and racks which showed from outside. Specially lit, whatever was inside had an added allure that made the rich and powerful look twice and go in. Once in, she would use her experience to make them buy from her array of art pieces. After you came before her in that art shop, you were at her mercy. She did not need to go to school for salesmanship, she told herself. She plotted it at home. There was no difference between a good salesperson and an experienced woman, she told herself. Seduction is a form of salesmanship and salesmanship is a form of seduction. The woman's body has to be packaged like a product for sale. Both the woman's body and the product have prices. She felt as if she was doing one of her literature papers in her final year at the university.

Once somebody rich had come inside into her web, she came to take the person round and explained, as professionally as she could, the meaning of the different art works. She mesmerized the customer with a smattering of art terms such as abstract, stylized, naturalism, and cubism that he definitely did not know. After the unwitting customer had been further dazzled by the reflection of glasses, different shades of light on the works on display racks, she invited the unwary into her office, a comfortable shrine that men wanted to sit in for as long as possible. There, she assumed without being contradicted that her guest had to buy at least one work. In many cases she chose for them what they wanted.

The day the office, as she called the shop, was opened, she had second thoughts about continuing to be called and known as Mrs. Daro. She felt she had accomplished what she needed to with "Mrs. Daro" and could now throw the name into the trash basket. Dede was free to give the name to his wife or whomever he lived with now. Within five days of the shop's opening, two major papers—*The Daily News* and *The Concord*—carried the declaration in the Name Change section.

I, formerly known as Mrs. Franka Daro, now wish to be known and addressed as Chief (Ms.) Franka Udi. All former documents remain valid. Federal Government, Lagos State Government, corporations, parastatals, and the general public should take note of the name change.

She printed a luscious card to reflect her new status.

CHIEF (MS.) FRANKA UDI, BA (HONORS)
AFRICAN ART DEALER
& GENERAL CONTRACTOR
1960 BROAD STREET EXTENSION
LAGOS
(01) 266-6060 (phone)

She knew what the title of chief meant in the society—respect. She also wanted to make it known to all and sundry that she was single; hence Ms. Udi. There was a certain freedom and independence in Ms. and she loved it before her name. She liked the title of chief and the BA (Honours) before and after her name respectively. She just wanted people to know that she was not an ordinary woman with her university degree.

She dressed elegantly in either African or Western attires that fitted her so well she earned the compliments of men and women. She chose colours to match whatever she wore: dresses, head-tie, if necessary, handbags, and shoes. She also styled her hair to invite compliments. It often took more than eight hours for the hairdresser to have her special braids done.

She carefully selected her perfumes from duty-free shops. Obsession, Red, Opium, and Ananais were too loud for her; so she picked something subtle that would steal into a man's head and make him lose his senses so as to make his heart captive in her office. She preferred French perfumes for being sexy and provocative—when she passed, she left a desire that haunted men until they turned or came back to her. Once before her, such men were unable to leave without paying her the price she set for her product. She loved Chanel and Escape. She also loved Poison and Pleasure, wherever they came from.

There was something creative in the perfumes that she liked; their banner-seeking names. Imagine 'Escape,' 'Poison,' 'Opium,' 'Red,' and 'Obsession.' There's surely much in a name, more so with perfumes; she told herself.

She found out that as Chief (Ms.) Franka Udi, she was more sought after and desired than before. Brigadier Otu's friend, Major-General Tango, to whom she had assigned Nkechi, was visiting her office and hauling away art works at any price she told him to pay. She sold him both "Women's Shadow" and "Diviner's Daughter," contemporary sculptures, and several abstract paintings and batiks. After all, he came with no specific image in mind and she had to make up his mind for him.

Many bosses, chief executives of their companies, came personally to the Art Shop instead of sending subordinates. They wanted to be in her presence, wanted to inhale her sexy fragrance, look with longing at her half-exposed breasts, and chat with her. They knew they had not much work to do in their offices anyway.

The Daily News, President Ogiso's official mouthpiece, ran a three-day piece on African art. The newspaper encouraged heads of departments to decorate their offices with products of Chef (Ms) Franka Udi's art shop, praised as the most visible source of genuine African art in the world.

The Governor of the Federal Bank that oversaw all the banks in the country came to her "office" to personally make purchases of the best available artworks to enhance the inside appearance of the bank's headquarters. After that deal had been struck, he promised to award her the contract of printing next year's calendar with artworks. The contract was worth ten million naira. However, the bank governor would receive four million from her as his share. To her, it was a great kill that could not be matched by anything she had done since becoming a full time art dealer and contractor. She sub-contracted it to a private printer in Ajegunle, showing him the artworks to use in depicting each month, for 500,000 naira. The printer, who had previously not done anything beyond printing church and wedding programs and obituaries, was happy to have a windfall. The shoddy work he did was discarded as not presentable, but she still received her pay. As part of the contract, she secretly provided the Governor of the Federal Bank the treat of his life at his secret guest house by the beach in Victoria Island.

Franka Udi became very rich within a year of owning the art shop. She built a house for herself in the exclusive Victoria Island area by the beach. To buy the land alone she spent ten million naira and that was a special deal because of its location. The land was a playground on the city map, but the state commissioner allocated it to her at a paltry ten million naira instead of twenty-five million that such land was going for. The plan of her house, a country home of nine large rooms, each with a bath and a toilet, was brought from England. A government contractor built it for her for assisting him to obtain the contract for the construction of a ten-kilometre road. The cost of building her mansion was added to the road contract. The building stood like a ship as it grew wider upwards. It was lavishly decorated with expensive furniture that met her high taste. This soon became the venue for parties for top military officers and their cronies. The brigadiers and generals came there evenings and nights to have pepper soup, get drunk, fondle women, and throw away the money they had stolen from the national coffers.

She was now a big employer. To do the cooking, she hired the mothers of the young women that she fixed up with her male guests. These older women were tucked inside the mansion and could not be seen by the visiting officers. She claimed she and her girlfriends did the cooking and received the compliments of the infatuated men.

The secret service infiltrated the events in the house in order to be sure that no coup plots were hatched under the guise of seeking women or relaxing with pepper soup and beer. The army often overlooked the sexual escapades of the officers and men, who often joked that "khaki no be leather" to describe their sexual cravings that needed to be filled.

Franka prospered from her wealth of experience. She attended a party at Government House with Brigadier Otu and shook hands with President Ogiso, who invited her to visit him sometime soon.

22

It was Brigadier Otu who kept reminding Franka of the president's invitation that she should visit him.

"Dear, he never forgets," he told her.

He stopped calling her Franka when she started calling him Gene.

"Are you sure he was not joking, just being pleasant to one of his guests at the party?" she asked him.

"Not the General," said Brigadier Otu. "He always means what he says."

"Don't worry, Gene. I'll go when I want to," she told the brigadier.

"You had better go soon before he reminds me of your promise to visit him," he said, as one who knew his commander-in-chief very well.

She could not understand why Brigadier Otu was so naive and so insistent on the president's invitation. She had seen President Ogiso's eyes overflowing with desire when they shook hands at the party in Government House. What does a cock skirt round a hen for, other than to fill its desire? She intuitively knew these things as a woman, an experienced one at that.

She decided to call on the president on a Friday afternoon. She had planned it in such a way that she would not have to spend a long time with him, since government offices closed at 1 p.m. that day nationwide. Surprisingly, unlike other visitors, she was ushered in like a familiar guest without search or questioning. The stern-faced guards gave her the salute, as if she were a senior officer in the Army. She did not know how to respond and just walked on.

It was as if the president was expecting her. He was sitting in a sofa on the other side of his huge mahogany office desk and looked relaxed,

129

contrary to her expectation of a tense man. If she were the commander-in-chief of this nation, she would not sleep and would carry the anxiety on her face. Either he was so confident of himself or he did not understand the hourly dangers he had to cope with, she thought.

He wore a general's uniform with its medals and appeared rather impressive in it. He wore his trademark dark goggles even in the office. There was no appearance of his being busy, and she thought that he might be already tidying his office to leave for the day.

"Why did you not come in one of your Oxford Street dresses?" he asked her.

Franka was dressed in a flowing embroidered *boubou*, a dress that was fashionable with high society women. She had no time to acclimatize herself to the cold air of the big office, nor could she look around, before the president's attack. Generals really surprise you. They prosper on ambushing their opponents. However, she did not see herself as the general's possible opponent. She regained her composure, smiled, and curtsied to him.

"I like this dress," she told him.

"I am just teasing you, but I have many eyes though. You look great in this, more like a queen than a chief," he told her.

"Thank you, Mr. President," she replied to the compliment.

She knew from the moment she left home what she was going for. A woman leaving home for such a goodwill visit had to prepare for all eventualities. There was nothing the president was going to consult her on that she could think of. After all, she was not a political scientist, nor was she one of the many armchair commentators and pundits on state television who always praised the president in the hope that he would notice them and offer them lucrative appointments.

In her mind, he surely wanted to have a feeling of success in all angles. Ruling with an iron fist was not enough for this man. Having so much money was not enough. Nor was decreeing his desires for the nation to obey enough power for him! He wanted more for his power to be absolute. He had to sleep with every woman he fancied before feeling fulfilled. It did not matter whether the woman was already married. Nor did it matter if she was already attached, however loosely, as she was, to Brigadier Otu. He must consummate his power with continuous intercourse with fresh women. Such men, as the general, saw sex with women as a form of domination that made them feel truly powerful, she thought. Maybe a dictator is a more complex personality than the public often thinks. She had no other way of interpreting the invitation.

Once the invitation was extended to her, she knew that eventually she had to go, regardless of whether or not Brigadier Otu reminded her. She knew that the dictator could send his agents to bundle her up and bring her to him, if she failed to heed his call. The hunter and the game have their own separate aims that guide their actions. It is fun for the game, if it is not afraid of a fatal shot from the hunter. She knew that once she could successfully win over the president, she herself would exercise power over the entire nation. She would lull the leopard to sleep and learn its secrets of power, de-fang it, if possible, for it to do her bidding. She did not come to do her national service in the president's office, but to exact a big price that a president's dignity could afford.

Recently she had taken pride in her experience and smartness. But little did she know that behind the perennial dark goggles of President Ogiso was a wily man of the world. By the time she left the president, who had forgotten two of his prayers, her head had been in the clouds. She had not thought that she would spend six hours with the president. She came in daylight; she went home by night. She declined his offer of one of his own state chauffeurs to drive her home. She came in her Mercedes Benz car and preferred driving herself home. She did not want anybody, general, president, or brigadier, to control her life. At least, that was how she felt when she could exercise her personal freedom.

What transpired between them was a secret. She now understood what mystified her as a child when elders told her about *Oku*. As a child she was told many commandments about Oku. What the eyes see at Oku must not be talked about. What the ears hear at Oku must not be exposed. What the hands touch at Oku must not be brought to the limelight. The Presidential Mansion was itself the Oku, a place of secrets. She had shared a conclave with the president.

The labyrinths of the compound intrigued her. He took her through a tunnel that led directly from his office to one of his guest houses. Despite the light, the tunnel had an eerie look about it. She felt at a time that she was buried alive, but that feeling left when they climbed up into one of the houses.

If she was dead, she was back to a startling new life. She could not piece things together as she saw a confusing network of tunnels. She could not summon up courage to ask about where the many tunnels led. He must have elaborate plans for his safety. There was only one way in, but many secret ways out. What a rabbit's hole the complex was! She exclaimed quietly.

He used another tunnel to take her to the house of gold, where the nation's gold reserve was kept, according to her escort. It glittered and he smiled profusely and beat his chest and said, "All this is ours." She did not know whom he meant by "ours," the entire people of the huge nation or just himself and his consorts.

She had not fully regained her normal vision after being dazzled by gold before he took her out. In another direction underground was a warehouse of money with freshly printed fifty naira notes. He carried the keys in his pocket. Here she was so overwhelmed that she bent down and fell on her knees to touch the money to see whether it was real naira notes or ordinary paper. Her mind ran riot.

Here was the money she had needed since her adolescent days for her education and sustenance. Here was the money that she had been seeking with a vengeance since her divorce to live well and to wipe out the shame from false accusations. Here was money that everybody in the nation hankered after; here was money that people were ready to die for. She had promised herself several years ago that she would step over death if possible to get to where money was. It looked so simple here. She did not hesitate to take wads of the large denomination into her roomy handbag when the president asked her to have a bite of the national cake, which she understood to mean that she should take as much of the money as she could carry away.

It was at the house of money that the president, who asked her to simply call him General, discussed her art shop and its transformation to the National Art Company with her as Director and General Manager. He was to have fifty percent of the shares; the remaining shares were hers. They toasted their split-even company with champagne, and each had good cause to be very happy at the events of that Friday.

Franka was surprised that the general did not suggest having an affair with her. Was he a gentleman or just biding his time till much later? Could a dictator have the finesse not to ask a lady guest for sex in their first real encounter? She realized that once in the Presidential Mansion, there was little resistance she could put up. She would wait and see whether her charm would not knock out the general.

Within two weeks of her first visit to the President, Franka got a big house donated by the government for the National Art Company. She visited the president two other nights in the office. He deliberately stayed in the office till very late in the evening to receive her on both occasions. Things started to happen as in fairy tales. In the second night call, he described the new site of the company to her and told her that she would be taken there when it was ready. Meanwhile, according to the general, her current "office" would be given a facelift.

The following day, she saw that it had been painted all white with a conspicuous signpost emblazoned with ART SHOP in glittering colours. How did they get the keys to go in and paint the inside? But her surprise would not end.

The next day racks and glass cases of a superior brand were already installed. Nobody saw anybody working there, but by each day there was a tremendous amount of work done. What surprised her the most was to get to work one morning and see a sign in her art shop: "CONVERTED TO NATIONAL ART COMPANY. NOW OPEN WITH NEW MANAGEMENT AT 2020 BROAD STREET." After all the renovations that took place in the old shop? she questioned herself. But she knew that money to spend was not the general's problem. She would no longer be surprised at anything after these dreamlike happenings.

A guard in an unidentifiable uniform told her to go to her new office. As if under a spell, she did not ask him who he was and who sent him there. But she knew that it was President Ogiso's hands working everything. The general worked like a spirit. She entered her Baby Benz and drove down the street to the site of her new office.

Everything was arranged as she could not have done herself. She stood with her mouth open and lacking words to express herself, as she stared at the filled shop. Her own works could not have made up to a tenth of what she saw before her. Here were woven clothes from Borno, Nupe beads and plates, Amo pots, Ikot Ekpene masks, Kerekere sculptures, Mumuye figures, Sokoto woven slippers, Oshogbo *adire*, Benin and Ife sculptures, and more. The items were uncountable. The foreign posters had disappeared to give more room for large photographs of national historical and geographical landmarks, including the Ikogosi Hot Springs, the confluence of the Benue and the Niger Rivers near Lokoja, the Obudu Ranch, Yankari Game Reserve, Gembu Wild Life, and a Kano tannery. What she saw was capable of making tourism a major foreign exchange earner for the country.

There was another uniformed man, who showed her the new office. The big table with the chair was a replica of the president's own desk. She ran her right palm over the special Formica that made the table shine. Now that she saw the new place, she was happy at her promotion from a mere art seller and dealer to the Director and General Manager of the National Art Company with equal shares with the president.

Brigadier Otu was surprised at her sudden rise to a superstore general manager. He felt uneasy before her new confidence. For the first time he addressed her as chief.

"Chief, how did you do all these without informing me? I would have chipped in something," he told her.

"It is your fault," she answered.

"How?" he asked, as someone surprised.

"That is not for me to answer. Maybe General will do that for me. You made a fool of yourself," she told him.

There was a new edge to her voice that frightened the brigadier. He suddenly realized that President Ogiso had taken over his girlfriend and he had better be careful about his own life. The general would clear him out of his way, and he had to look for a way out. In the National Army, however, there was no way out of General Ogiso's trap. He would wait and see whether taking her from him would be enough for the president.

Within three days of her occupying her new office at the National Art Company, there was a snap announcement on the Federal Military Government-controlled national radio and television networks of promotions in the Army. Eugene Otu was one of the five brigadiers who were elevated to the rank of major-general. He was elated and planned to celebrate after his official decoration with a red eaglet pip and three stars on his uniform.

The plan for the party was interrupted by another announcement several days later. This concerned a shuffle of ambassadors and the re-deployment of new and old ones. The president, according to his secretary, had not been pleased by the performance of many of his envoys. They had been unable to promote a positive image of the country abroad and had failed woefully to attract tourists and investments from the developed nations. He needed new ambassadors to bring about a change from the nation's poor image to something that would be a pride to all.

In the replacements that followed, Major-General Eugene Otu was posted to Pakistan as High Commissioner "with immediate effect". He knew army procedure meant he had to leave immediately, but he was full of suspicions. How was Pakistan going to help in the economic development when it was as underdeveloped as his country? This must be a sinister move, he felt. General Ogiso had not forgotten his careless talk after he seized power. Otu had stated that he, Ogiso, would not survive three months in office. That was many years ago. How the general got to know about his statement could only confirm that the president had as many eyes as ears, and they were paid to be very sharp and alert.

The president had continued to promote him from his previous rank of lieutenant colonel, as well as some others whose loyalty he could not count on, to appear fair to everybody. He smiled at his imagined foes, even as he schemed to hurt them. One of his praise names was Crocodile. He knew how to be very patient at seizing the opportunity to destroy his enemy. He did not forget any personal insult or affront and waited all the time it took to pay back. If Eugene Otu thought he was off the hook on his statement of seven years ago, he was quite mistaken.

Major-General Eugene Otu was denied entrance to Chief (Ms.) Franka Udi's house at the beach in Victoria Island when he went to visit her. Three soldiers on guard stood there to shield the house from intrusion. In normal times, such soldiers on guard duty could not deny a major-general entrance to a place, but he saw that times had changed. He did not protest to Franka. He went home to pack his things in preparation for the long flight to Islamabad in Pakistan.

The general had promised her many things, she knew. Barely three months as Director and General Manager of the National Art Company, there was a surprise. She woke one morning and heard her name called in a special bulletin on a cabinet reshuffle so frequent in General Ogiso's rule. He did not allow any of his ministers to hold one portfolio for too long, the same way he redeployed his commanders to pre-empt any plot.

She turned the radio louder to hear the special announcement. The general had told her to expect a big gift on her birthday, and she was thinking of money or gold from those vaults. Was he waiting to give her this special gift before expressing his desire for her, or the gift itself would be an expression of his romantic intention? After the usual preamble of the need for new blood to revitalize the government and the streamlining of ministries to give maximum efficiency, the new ministers' names were called and their respective portfolios announced. There was to be a new Minister of Information and Culture, Chief Franka Udi. She would be directly responsible to the president on matters of culture and information, unlike others who had to go through the Chief of General Staff. This was because, according to the Secretary to the Government, the country was suffering terribly from a negative image that must be replaced immediately with a positive one.

Franka was sworn in three days later, about the very moment that Major-General Otu was boarding the plane on his long journey to assume his new posting. The swearing-in ceremony of the new ambassadors had been postponed thrice because the president had other pressing duties that kept him away. As Minister of Information and Culture, Franka had become the mouthpiece of the Federal

Military Government. Like those who held the post before her, all she had to do was sing the praises of the government. Her thirty-something birthday was a landmark in her life. In the emotions of the time, she had forgotten how old she was. That did not matter now, she felt. She was a capable lady in many aspects and she would prove herself capable of being a successful minister.

She was tucked in the labyrinth of the State House, a huge complex that could barely be seen from outside. Those who went to parties there only saw a fraction of the place. From the beginning, President Ogiso did not plan the housing complex to be seen fully from a distance. He re-modelled and renovated the complex to suit his security and other personal needs. Maybe that was why many mansions that made up the State House complex were built to look alike. He was looking forward to Abuja, where caves were to be part of the new State House complex.

Now known as Honourable Chief Franka Udi, with the Ms. dropped, she had her living quarters close to the president's own living place. She had never stepped into a more opulent house than what she now occupied. Her personal house was luxurious, but not to the extent of this State House quarters. The proximity of her bungalow gave the general the privilege of calling on her at home at any time he wished.

She knew she had to be quiet, as one experiencing life in Oku, over the many strange visitors, diviners, and medicine men that were brought to the president's own quarters. Many nights she saw goats, rams, fowls, chimpanzees, or figures that looked human slaughtered as sacrifices to spirits to protect the general from his enemies. From their appearances and dress styles, some of the marabous and medicine men came from as far away as Mali, Sudan, and Egypt.

As for herself, she would cultivate her body to bring her what she wanted. She was confident she could charm these medicine men. She still used her French perfumes, which she felt were more potent charms than what these native doctors prepared for General Ogiso.

23

The State Secret Service and other government security agencies had been monitoring Dede Daro more closely since the NAD scare. They read his writings, followed his appearances and talks, and stalked him sometimes openly and at other times discreetly. In addition to the many professional agents that were more than a fifth of the civil service, the government pursued vigorously the recruitment of informers among students and those who worked in the press. It felt these were strategic to catching early any dissidents that wanted to do mischief. University teachers and students and the press did not shut their mouths, or did not know how to keep secrets. The government wanted to impress on its critics that they were being watched all the time. With such knowledge and craft, the government was hopeful that it would stay in power for as long as it took to accomplish its goals, which defined themselves day by day. It would take the necessary time, no matter how long, to accomplish its lofty ideals of a peaceful state, even if that state became a cemetery.

In recent months Dede had been elected into the executive committee of the National Forum for Democracy (NAFORD). It was an umbrella union of many human rights organizations with a central coordinating secretariat. Most often, the smaller organizations did not have the financial wherewithal and the professional expertise to be as effective as their goals promoted. There was rivalry to gain attention at home and abroad, but it soon dawned on many of the groups that they had a common enemy that they should face with a unified strategy. A new day was definitely dawning, with the opposition intensifying against the military government.

The Forum had openly called on General Ogiso to step down for party elections. It also now called for a week of national mourning to be marked by a stay-at-home for workers. Strikes were officially illegal, banned by a military decree; hence the euphemism of stay-at-home, which everybody understood to be a call for a national strike. As a symbolic gesture, the week would start on October 1, a Friday and run through the next Thursday.

The government was enraged. October 1, the national day, was close at hand. It interpreted the call for a strike as a guise for an opposition conspiracy to subvert the national day celebration. That day, the president always addressed the nation in a live broadcast in his ceremonial dress with all his medals on his chest. In recent years, citing security reasons, the outdoor activities of the special day had been scaled down. The president was eager to cancel any ceremony that he saw as posing security risks. With what had happened to President Anwar Sadat in Egypt decades ago, it would be reckless to have him review a military parade on that day. One has to learn from experience, the secret agents advised him. The broadcast remained the major event of the national day. If the strike took place, it could cast a dark shadow over the whole ceremony and the image of the country, which he wanted to polish into a special brilliance.

At first he offhandedly dismissed the threat of a strike called a week of national mourning. He was quoted as saying that whoever liked could go on strike for the remaining period of their lives because that would not affect him.

"Are my children coming to your schools? Will my sick mother come to your hospital? Am I going to fly in your planes?" he yelled at his cabinet.

"No, Mr. President," the ministers chorused.

He liked his ministers to address him as Mr. President.

"How many traps in the air will catch the eagle?" he asked, unsure of the implication of comparing himself to an eagle, the totemic bird after which the national airline was named.

He did not pause to give them the opportunity to answer his question. As was the practice, nobody interrupted the president.

"My ministers, I'll leave this to you. Let me know how you can control the situation and bring calm," he said.

"Can't the so-called week of national mourning be aborted?" Chief Franka Udi asked.

"You all should put your heads together and deal with the situation accordingly," he ordered.

The government threatened to fire all workers who refused to report for work. The people were used to being fired at the whims and caprices of their leaders, so being fired from jobs that not only paid inadequate wages but whose workers were owed several months' salaries would not scare them enough to change their minds.

Support grew for the week of national mourning. A week to the day, the NAD agreed to show solidarity for the patriotic struggle by joining the groups about to demonstrate before Government House in all the states and the federal capital. The national labour union, an umbrella organization of many unions, as well as many other groups also pledged to "mourn" for the nation because the country's hope at independence was dying and it was needless to celebrate one more year of military rule. Rather, every patriotic citizen should "mourn" the lost potentials of the nation that had been destined to be a shining star, but that had become a dark blot on the continent's map.

Dede's "matters of the moment" had become more frequent and regular. Now the column appeared on Mondays and Fridays. He felt his countrymen and women were still sleeping or having a nauseating hangover by Monday morning, so they needed to be awakened properly to begin their workweek. Friday's column gave the readers something to keep them from forgetting the national disease during the weekend. Memory was important in the effort to free oneself from a tyranny, he calculated.

Now he conceived of a daily "matter of the moment" Monday through Friday, and covering October 1. Pressure was what scared the "uniformed jackals," his new term for the president and his livery of gun-carrying praise-singers. Pressure from within and without. Whatever pressure the international body mounted against a dictatorship as deeply entrenched as the Ogiso junta, the internal pressure must first undermine from the base within for it to topple over. He believed that not through armed struggle alone could the military dictatorship be overthrown; there were other means. He would end the week before the crucial week of national mourning with a reflection on power.

So on Friday, September 24, he fired the first shot.

Notions of Power

These are very desperate times we live in. There is famine across the country, especially in rural areas. Rinderpest is bringing down the cow population. Crops are failing from the havoc done by beetles and locusts. Diseases are rampant and there are no hospitals to care for the sick. Diseases such as polio, tuberculosis, and smallpox thought long eradicated worldwide have resurfaced in the land as well as new and strange diseases without known cures. AIDS is the new plague. Add these scourges to the gun and you can see the gravity of the national plight.

Nobody breathes the air of freedom in the perennially humid atmosphere. It is a miracle that we survive under these excruciating circumstances. Some will therefore argue that in these hard and desperate days we do not need to engage in flights of fancy. But such people should excuse me for this one flight only.

In my undergraduate days, I took a course in Romantic Poetry. I was expecting a lot of romance after being used by big girls in my secondary school to write love letters for them to their boyfriends. I expected a lot of romance to prepare me for the world outside of books. The "romance" of these poets was not what I wanted; in fact, the content of the course was very unromantic. Up to this day, I find it difficult to understand why these poets, except for the strange Byron, are called Romantic. I must confess that white folks have a knack for weird things and are prone to exaggerate; hence they might see romantic aspects in trees, rivers, and lakes.

Unromantic as these poets seemed to me, that course became one of the most rewarding in my university life. One of the few poems I frequently go back to is P.B. Shelley's "Ozymandias." I recommend the poem to everybody for its indelible lessons.

Today's "matter of the moment" is the abuse and misuse of power across the land. Power has become an intoxicating berry, which once eaten hooks its consumer to an insatiable appetite. It breeds an incurable addiction. This sweet fruit lifts its consumers into an inhuman plane. There and then they become primitive giants who mindlessly trample humans underfoot. The lives of others have no value and only their own selfish desires for more inordinate power count. Some exercise power to level poor people's homes to create space for the rich to build mansions on, as we witnessed in Maroko. There is power to shoot at peaceful demonstrators, as was done in the Niger Delta. Others see power as an opportunity to arrest the disabled. There is power to rape other people's wives, as there is also power to steal from or rob the community's coffers and squander the wealth on trifles. Many exercise their power to break laws with impunity. The powerful even believe they can arrest people's thoughts and yearnings for freedom and happiness.

Hurting others makes the power-drunk more delirious. They daub their foreheads with the blood of their imagined enemies and smile contentment to themselves in the island homes they had built and now live in. Snatching the leftovers of their rich tables from the hands of the starving populace makes them ecstatic. When one abuses power, one

140

abuses every virtue that humanity holds dear. The irony of it is that they feel they want to meet their human needs. It is not human to be inhumane; it will never be human to live the life of a beast.

Now let's go back to "Ozymandias." Let the rich, titled, and powerful build monuments out of the sweat of slaves. Ancient Benin did it and attributed the feat to Arhuaran, a giant. Ancient Zimbabwe did it and attributed it to the wisdom of a chief. Let them build skyscrapers to pierce the sky. Let them cruise the skies with their private jets and think they are having a foretaste of heaven on earth. Let them boast of the largest, tallest and biggest sculptures of their images on earth. Let their names be cast in stone or marble. The law of nature will prevail over all as it did with Ozymandias. Only rubble and sand, an expanse of dust, will be left of the bloated egos that parade themselves in the finest of cars. Nothing will remain. Ozymandias's experience should be a humbling lesson to all. A lifetime is too short to stand against humanity. All human talents and energy should be geared towards enriching the humanity that we are born into. The least we can demand of the powerful is for them to use power to benefit all humans. Let all victims of power come out and mourn our plight. Today we are all victims.

There were limits the president did not want crossed. You could fire tirades against social ills, against corruption, and not be a threat. He had "eyes" and "ears" in the production line of *The African Patriot* and so knew what transpired there. The tirade on power was an academic exercise and most readers, the government believed, would not understand Dede's essay. But to call on people to come out en masse in solidarity for the national day of mourning demonstration on October 1, as the paper's editorial did, crossed the line.

Still the president bided his time. An experienced general did not hurry into war. He took time to plan and to surprise his enemy. A surprise attack from nowhere always helped. He possessed the patience of the crocodile. He would wait for the opportune time and even weep profuse tears like the crocodile, after swallowing its victim. He advised his overzealous agents not to hasten to arrest or do harm to the journalist who was a big thorn in his flesh. For once, it occurred to him at the briefing that Chief Udi was once the journalist's wife, but he said nothing about it. The proposed attack should be as indirect as possible.

"No personalities, just our security," he told his cabinet.

"Yes sir, Mr. President," they replied.

They did not quite understand what he meant, but they could not admit not understanding his orders. That would make all of them incompetent and another excuse for a cabinet reshuffle. Something had to be done. At least something had to be tried to impress him that they were hardworking men and women around him. They did not want to be perceived otherwise.

Another decree was promulgated to reinforce the banning of groups from demonstrating. No group should demonstrate for or against anybody or the government. Such groups that demonstrated would be dissolved. The lengthy decree also warned individuals not to use their positions and offices to incite insurrection against the government, and threatened that those who chose to break the laws of the land would pay dearly for it. Such harsh language had worked well in the past to scare people off the streets and the president and his cabinet hoped it would do the same this time.

They were mistaken. The executive committees of many associations, including those of the NAD and the NAFORD, issued statements that their protests would go ahead as planned. They argued that rejecting the inhuman decrees of a dictatorial and illegal regime was not the same thing as breaking the laws of the land. Rather, it was the decrees that broke the laws of the people of the land. They went on to analyze the national situation for those in power who did not seem to understand the national debacle. This national day was the thirty-fifth anniversary of the country's independence. The nation was no longer young. How old must a nation be to have a sense of direction? One has to prepare for old age, Dede implied. A country's affairs are like the life of an individual, and responsibility is very important.

24

A few days before the day of national mourning, on Monday, September 27, the unexpected struck. Tetebe had a serious crisis, which Dede's parental experience could not help to manage. At five years, she appeared normal for a child of her age. Her father was to drop her at St. Anthony's Nursery School early in the morning when she started crying and groaning. The groaning intensified as they drove closer to the school. Her eyes suddenly became swollen and half-closed, her lips shaky, and her whole body hot. High fever along with a crisis had not come at the same time with her before now.

Dede made up his mind instantly to drive straight to the hospital for Dr. Laoye to examine her. He knew that he might miss a crucial meeting of the editorial board on the national day issue that morning. There was already an agreement for the paper to have a blank black front page. The symbolism would be clear to every reader. The back cover story that would suit this best would be one of his "matters of the moment" pieces, which he had already submitted to Ena Tobore to read before the meeting.

"Averting National Suicide" would make the one-page editorial. The short piece was about not keeping silent in the face of tyranny, since doing otherwise was a sure way to facilitate the downfall of a country. One should not allow a leopard and its cubs to terrorize the land. Let the other animals use their wit to bring down their tormentor. The small animals that are possible victims of the leopard could catch the monstrous animal asleep and deal it a deathblow. If all fowls united, the hawk would not succeed in snatching a single one away. It is only when broomsticks are tied together that they sweep clean.

Though everything was in place for the special issue of the paper, it was still not all right for him to miss the meeting. He would do his possible best to have Tetebe taken to the hospital and still attend the paper's meeting to make his contribution to the discussion.

Going towards Lagos Mainland at 7:30 in the morning was swimming against a racing current. One had to be alert and patient. Slowly, and with his attention divided between his sick daughter and the many brainless drivers of the early morning commute, he made it to the hospital in two hours. Dr. Laoye had been attending to some other children whose cases were serious. The nurses took Tetebe into a consultation room, took her temperature and blood pressure in preparation for the doctor's arrival. The doctor soon came to attend to her.

Dr. Laoye had the tact of an able physician. He knew it was an extremely bad case. By now, Tetebe's eyes were swollen big and she looked very pale. The doctor was calm and methodical, so as not to make the parent panic. He knew he had to be reassuring to both the patient and the family. After examining the little girl, he asked the nurses to admit her into one of the vacant beds. The girl's temperature was dangerously high.

"She will need to be closely monitored," he told Dede.

"That's fine with me," he answered.

"She may have to be here for some days. I think she's developed pneumonia and perhaps asthma with an acute crisis," the doctor further explained to the worried parent.

"She's now under your care," he told him.

He had absolute confidence in Dr. Laoye, one of the few doctors dedicated to their patients. Dr. Laoye had no private clinic to which he referred his patients, as many other doctors did. He was always ready on call and served with selfless devotion. Dede trusted him and felt that his daughter couldn't be under better care anywhere.

"Let's watch her. Such a case as hers changes so often," the doctor said, as he adjusted his stethoscope hanging from his neck.

"I want to go and tell Furu what's happening. She doesn't know we are here. I have to go to her school to tell her. After informing her, I'll go to my paper to briefly sit at a meeting and then come back," Dede told the doctor.

"Try to be back as soon as you can. We'll do our best for her," Dr. Laoye assured him.

Furu had a mystical attachment to her daughter. During the later months of her pregnancy, once she became hungry, the baby started kicking. Then she slept on her back and woke at about six as the baby pressed her by the left side. She did not need an alarm clock to wake to prepare for school. As Tetebe grew up, whenever something was going wrong with her, Furu knew instinctively. She had woken up at night unexpectedly to notice that her daughter had a fever and acted on it immediately. She had told Dede that whatever hurt Tetebe afflicted her too. She suffered from pains, she said, that were extensions of her daughter's and she bore them well.

As soon as she saw Dede, after being called to the staff room, she had a feeling that something was wrong with their daughter. Nothing else she could imagine would bring him to see her when he knew she was busy teaching.

"What's wrong with Tete?" she asked.

She called her daughter Tete for short and stressed the two syllables of the name.

"She suddenly took ill and I had to take her to the hospital," he told her.

"Where's she now?" she asked.

"She's still in the hospital."

"You should have come to collect me to go with you," she complained.

"I had to drive straight there because she was writhing in pain as never before," he explained.

"Let's go back to the hospital," she ordered.

"I wanted to pass by my paper to apologize for not attending a meeting," he told her.

"Your paper will take care of itself. Let's go back to the hospital to see Tete. When you've dropped me, you can go there, if you must," she said.

He rarely saw her firm, and once she was determined like this regarding their daughter's health, he knew that he should not contradict her. She was firm and serious and would not accept any other answer than going straight to Tetebe. He thought about it. Yes, his office work was important, but his daughter's health was paramount. It was an emergency, which demanded attention and every boss would understand the situation.

He drove fast. There was anxiety weighing heavily on Furu's mind and one could tell from her gaze that she was deep in thought. This time the road was much freer than in the early morning. Most people had already arrived at work. As they drove to the hospital, they were silent in anticipation of their daughter's condition and soon arrived at their destination.

Dr. Laoye and the nurses had been waiting for them. Tetebe's blood count was very low, the percentage of the sickling corpuscles eighty-five percent, just too high. The girl was still in serious pain. In his many years of practice attending to sickle cell patients, the doctor knew that after the first two years, the age of five, as with Tetebe, was crucial. These signs were precursors of a stroke that could result in the death of the child or her being crippled for life. Whatever the outcome of a stroke, it was often bleak.

He recommended massive blood transfusion. That would restore the corpuscles to a regular state. That would remove the possible blood clot and also bring into her body enough oxygen for her to recover.

Furu hated the idea of paying the homeless or strangers for pints of blood. They were always around by the hospital gate driving a hard bargain as to how much they should be paid. Almost like vultures waiting for cadavers, they prayed for people to be seriously sick to need their services. But at the same time she sympathized with them because they needed money and did not mind selling their own blood for it. She preferred those who sold their blood for sustenance to those who robbed, and the country was full of different types of robbers.

"We have to give our blood," Furu told Dede.

"If ours will match hers," he said.

"I think hers is type O positive," she said.

"You know we only tested ours to confirm we have sickle cell trait, but have not checked our blood type," he responded.

"Let's hope it will match hers," she said, as if in prayer.

After the brief consultation between them, the partners came to Dr. Laoye to tell him that they would give their blood for the transfusion. The doctor bit his lips and shook his head. He was used to seeing highly educated parents ignorant about problems of their sickle cell children. Much needed to be done in public enlightenment about health problems. Parents should be educated about paediatric ailments and how to treat them.

"As much as possible the blood of the parents of sicklers is not used for transfusion. You have to understand that you carry traits and she will need blood that is totally free of any sickles or the trait," he told his patient's parents.

They both understood and wondered why they had been so dumb as not to know this.

"I have to go outside then to look for somebody to buy blood from," Furu said.

It was almost one o'clock and the first shift of nurses was leaving as the second shift took over. Outside the hospital's gate, the men selling their blood loitered for seekers of their specific blood types. They wore banners of their blood types to be easily identified. Usually haggling went on for five or more minutes to get the best bargain of the lot. Some needy people went for the healthiest looking person selling blood and did not care for the price. Furu and Dede were saved from these desperate human predators.

Two nurses who had attended to Tetebe talked in a low voice to themselves. They followed Furu outside and called her as soon as they were out of the paediatric ward. They told her that they would not mind donating blood for her daughter's transfusion if the doctor would not object, since doctors tended to advise their nurses not to be too emotional about patients. When they volunteered their blood to be matched against Tetebe's, the other nurses were happily surprised that Dr. Laoye did not object. The doctor nodded his head as if in appreciation of their generosity.

Fortunately, the blood of the two nurses matched Tetebe's type O positive. Blood was drawn from both nurses for screening. Before they had rested for a half-hour, the result came. Their blood was free of any problems. Soon the transfusion started. Furu and Dede were very grateful to the nurses, who slipped away as the nurses on duty were doing their assigned responsibilities. They would learn that the two nurses belonged to the Sisters of Solace group that also volunteered on their free days to visit the sick in the hospital.

Furu sat by Tetebe's head, gazing at her eyes. She was sleeping and the doctor said that was normal and that she would wake stronger. Once Dede noticed things were under control, he told Furu that he was going home to see Uvie who had been with them for some months now, change his clothes, bring new ones for Furu, and get some money which they definitely needed.

Time had passed so fast. It was already three o'clock. As he drove back, he decided to take a route that would first take him to his newspaper offices before going to his house. Though this was a longer route, it saved him time because he would not need to go there from home before coming back to the hospital. Most of the administrative staff of *The African Patriot* closed at five but the offices were busy all day long. He hoped to catch the publisher and other members of the editorial board and learn what they had discussed at the meeting he missed. As soon as he went out of the hospital, he saw groups of people here and there talking in muted tones. In this country, gossip was a major hobby. More so on Mondays when happenings during the weekend dominated the conversations of workers. On Mondays too, new government policies and decrees were published and soon after midday offices buzzed with the latest in General Ogiso's proclamations. Besides, this was the first working day of the week that the planned national mourning would start.

As he drove closer to the offices of *The African Patriot*, he had a sense of foreboding. There were more clusters of gossiping people. He hoped that at his office he would find out if there was breaking news. From a distance, he saw men in police and army uniforms. They were apparently on the premises of *The African Patriot*. Then he noticed one of the office attendants, David Agbogidi, frantically waving him to stop. He pressed hard on his brakes, as if to avoid running over somebody. He did not need to be told that there was bad news.

He knew it was something terrible from the way David placed his hands over his head. Had *The African Patriot* been shut down by President Ogiso or his new minister of information and culture? What was the latest decree on, that the newspaper had to be taken over by a detachment of army and police?

"They've killed our Publisher," David muttered through sobs.

Dede was shocked.

"Go back, or they will arrest or kill you too," he advised him.

He was confused but had to make up his mind instantly. He was torn between a public confrontation with the armed forces, no matter the consequence, and joining his family at a crucial time. He did not have to choose to go one way or the other, but knew it would be foolhardy to enter into the iron grip of the army and police, Ogiso's loyalist forces. He needed to know what was happening to better react to the situation. He felt lucky that David had stopped him before he came too close to his office. He asked David to get into the car and, rather than go ahead, he turned instead to drive towards his home.

"If I be you, I go run far far," David told him.

"Run to where?" he asked.

"Run anywhere far far. Na for your life," David explained.

"No, David. I can't run from my family," he said.

At home he heard about the blast that had instantly tore Ena Tobore into shreds and injured several members of the editorial board. His neighbours had heard and had been afraid he too might have been killed or injured. They had heard that up to five of the top officers of the paper were killed, but David confirmed that only Ena Tobore was killed. His neighbours had asked about his wife, as they called Furu, who was said to have left school suddenly on an emergency. That fuelled their fears for his safety. But Uvie was at home, unaware of either the blast in his father's workplace or of Tetebe's sudden illness. He walked to and from his school, which was nearby.

148

Dede took Uvie, the clothes he and Furu needed for the night, and some money he had at home and drove back to the hospital. He had to drop David at a place where he could easily take a bus to Mile Two, where he lived. He gave him twenty naira to pay the bus fare.

When he came back to the hospital, there was a clearer picture of what had happened. Furu had heard about the blast and was happy that Dede had not gone to the office earlier in the day. Some of Dede's colleagues had been brought to the hospital. He visited his wounded colleagues who had been first sent to the General Hospital from where their families and friends had then removed them to the Catholic Hospital.

Dede learned that a dispatch rider on a motorcycle wearing a helmet and a sort of uniform that could not be ascribed to any of the armed forces or security services had come to deliver a parcel. The dispatch rider had asked specifically for "Mr. Dede Daro, Publishing Manager, *The African Patriot*," to whom the parcel was addressed.

"Since you were not around," Matthew Igene, also of the editorial board, told him, "Ena felt it was meant for him, publisher and manager, and that it was a case of misdirection. He jokingly said 'I'll open it but won't read it if it's a love letter!' Then he began to rip open the parcel."

Dede covered his face with his palm. He mentally recreated the sitting arrangement at the editorial table. He usually took the opposite end from Ena Tobore, who sometimes joked that the two ends of the table were one mind because they had to agree unanimously on what they would publish.

"Then there was the loud blast," continued Matthew. "None of us there knew what happened immediately afterwards. For minutes there was confusion as everybody there was disoriented momentarily by the blast, before recovering with different degrees of injuries to scramble for safety in all directions. As we regained consciousness, we realized we had lost Ena. The impact of the blast had been such that he was torn to pieces. It was so direct that he had no chance of escaping the fatal injuries."

"What a tragedy!" Dede exclaimed.

"It's a great tragedy for all of us," Matthew said.

"What of the dispatch rider?" Dede asked.

"Nobody saw him afterwards, nor did the gate-men know where he fled to," Matthew answered.

There was a momentary silence as they reflected on what had happened.

"A piece of paper that must have been torn from a sheet contained three lines; in fact it was a title of what looked like a poem and two lines—I thought I read the title as "The Accusation." I dropped the piece as I left the premises, after police and army men came in and asked us to drop everything in our possession for them to gather evidence," Matthew further narrated.

Dede knew that the parcel bomb had been meant for him. How did his poem get out of his cabinet in the office? How could it have been seen and removed? There must be agents working in the office he did not suspect. Only he, the writer, knew of the poem, which he kept with other private writings in a special drawer in his cabinet. It was only now that he realized the magnitude of his personal risk. However, he felt bad that somebody else had died in his place.

He had known for more than a year that those people in uniforms that could not be ascribed to any of the armed forces were secret service agents of the government. They were more dangerous than the regular ones because they could not be identified or pinned down to an organization. But it was too late. It had never occurred to him that the government would attempt to kill him or anyone in the press with a parcel bomb. The government's practice in cracking down on its critics had been to detain and torture them in jail. There, detainees died of malaria or committed suicide, according to police reports. The government did not allow independent autopsies to be performed to ascertain the medical cause of deaths. Nobody believed the police reports that were all fabricated. Now the agents were getting more creative, sophisticated, and sinister in their methods of eliminating the junta's opponents without being directly seen as responsible. Government opponents were no longer being thrown into jail and never heard from again. That was too blatant. Also, the days of taking activists in flights from the island prison in military helicopters and dropping them into the Atlantic Ocean were gone.

Dede knew he owed a responsibility to the dead publisher and his family. But he would see through the night that his daughter improved. These transfusions had their problems, as Dr. Laoye had told him, but there was no cause for fear. He had a wakeful night keeping watch over Tetebe and thinking of his late friend and boss, Ena.

The following morning, a special government bulletin that was read on the radio and television conveyed sympathies to the family of Dr. Ena Tobore on his violent death, as it described it. It spoke of his heroic contribution to the cause of journalism in the country and that his place in the history of the press in the country would be difficult to fill. Dede knew this was a typical crocodile shedding tears; whoever killed Ena Tobore must be a part of the government, he believed.

In a rather sinister turn, the same bulletin also ordered the immediate closing of all independent newspapers. According to the statement, these papers had become centres of terrorist activities that would no longer be tolerated. The closure of these institutions, the government argued, was for the best interest of the general public. The Honourable Minister of Information and Culture, Chief Franka Udi, signed the statement for the president.

25

The burial rites of Ena Tobore fell on Wednesday, less than forty-eight hours to Independence Day and the start of the week of national mourning. Representatives of different national and international organizations came to St. Augustine's Church for the memorial service. Amnesty International, PEN International, the Pan-African Union of Journalists, and the Organization of African Trade Unions registered their presence. Some embassies also had their information officers or delegates to represent them as a protest against the military dictatorship, which they blamed for the veteran journalist's death.

The presence of many disabled, vendors of *The African Patriot*, and the paper's readers' club members who came to pay their last respects to a great citizen of the country deeply impressed Dede. Also present were relatives, friends, and community leaders. Many lecturers and students also came from the Universities of Lagos, Ife, Benin, and Ibadan to express their grief and solidarity with Ena Tobore's family, *The African Patriot*, and its staff.

Furu could not make it because of Tetebe who was still in hospital recovering from pneumonia and regaining her strength after the blood transfusion. The asthma had been successfully treated. She was being given some antibiotics to prevent any infections. Dede and his family had virtually camped at the paediatric ward for days. Since Uvie was with them in the hospital, they were able to stay away from home and together.

Dede had attended the wake in Ena Tobore's Ikeja residence the previous evening. There were religious songs and readings from Ena's articles written over three decades. Despite the cruel nature of his death, the wake was a celebration of his life. Refreshments were served. The casket was closed, perhaps to avoid displaying his dismembered body. Mourners filed past it in bowed respect.

On the day of the burial, Dede sat beside the bereaved family. After praying for the deceased's soul to rest in peace and sprinkling holy water over the bier, the priest called on Dede Daro to give the eulogy. He moved to the lectern in front. He wiped his face, looked toward the coffin of Ena Tobore, and wiped his face again.

"I should be the one in the coffin," he said in an outburst of tears.

He could remember his weeping only once before. That was when his grandmother who had raised him died. But now, he thought of his senior colleague who had died instead of him. Mrs. Tobore and their three children also burst into tears, followed by others. The priest, no doubt used to this type of behaviour, stood up from his chair, and coughed. The congregation understood this to be a plea for self-control and those who were crying stopped their loud wails.

"Again I say that Dr. Tobore died for me," Dede resumed. "However, today," he intoned, "we bury not only Dr. Tobore but all of us. Those who killed him should not be allowed to gain comfort that we can be silenced, intimidated, harassed, and killed, without responding against tyranny. The pressure must be intensified. The fire must be kindled beneath the murderers' behinds."

A woman at the back dressed in black started a wail, which triggered others and spread all over the huge church. Dede knew he had to pause to allow the mourners to express themselves. Then he continued.

"Ena, Ena, Ena! Only you there, now unassailable, can tell who felled the gigantic *iroko* tree that you have been in our midst. Our *iroko* has fallen! We weep because you have gone very far away, so far that neither a letter nor a telegram can reach you. We know that wherever you are, you will always be with us. The wind will always carry your voice through jungles of silence into our ears. Shake our ears with your orders. Dreams will bring you back to our midst in live appearances. Make us dream good and big dreams. Make us dream of true freedom and prosperity. You must come back because we need your third eye to overcome the lack of vision in the land. We are visually impaired and continue to grope for a sense of direction. We need all you stood for to free our land from the stranglehold of brutes. You must come back in a new army of upright ones to walk erect through the many crooked lanes around. You must smash the cycle of failures that we have been subjected to these three decades. I know that you are gone, but even there you are in another kind of army regrouping under the betrayed general of national hope to fight back. You must destroy the uniform that state executives now wear upside down. You must save us from your invisible end in the other world. God bless you, Dr. Tobore."

Everybody rose, no doubt moved by the poetry of the eulogy. After he finished, even the priest was dazed for a moment. People bowed in silence and in respect for the late publisher. When the priest had recovered himself, he turned to the choir to sing "Amazing Grace," whose lyrics further reinforced the solemn atmosphere.

A collection basket was passed round for Dr. Tobore's children. Many responded beyond expectation, and the priest thanked all those who had made contributions. After the offering and contribution, different groups were recognized; some read brief messages of condolences. At the end of the service, the priest again called on him, the Senior Editor, to make the closing remarks.

"It is a pity and a shame that the grounds of *The African Patriot* are occupied by the police and the army. The paper's grounds ought to be the last stop for Dr. Tobore before heading for the cemetery. Now he will be buried without reaching there. But he will be buried with the last seven issues of the paper and we who worked under him wish him a peaceful rest. Thank you all who have come to honour the memory of a great fighter for human rights. Peace," he concluded.

That evening, a crowd followed the publisher's body to the cemetery amidst songs and drums. The cortege moved slowly with dignity to the Mainland Cemetery, where he was laid to rest.

The government saw what was happening and felt relieved that the so-called week of national mourning had started with Dr. Tobore's funeral. One enemy was gone, even though not the desired target, the government knew in its relief and hope that the biting editorials of *The African Patriot* would, for now, be reduced.

26

It was late in the evening on Wednesday. The Presidential Mansion was a different world from the rest of Lagos. It felt nothing of the grief that had stricken the literate populace because of Ena Tobore's death. The many eyes and ears of state reported the newspaper manager's funeral, which did not douse the spirit of residents of the Presidential Mansion. Those there and on their side never felt the pain or grief as the rest of the nation.

Franka was used to expecting the general every other night, and today was her day. At the end of the day's work, she came home and collapsed into her favourite couch. She had been busier than normal in recent times. The cabinet had to deal with the national crisis of an impending workers' stay-at-home action. She was busy overseeing bulletins and crafting the wordings of decrees to deter enemies of the government from further escalating the already tense situation. She used her English and the little law that she had studied to her advantage in the generally half-literate cabinet. She was the unofficial legal adviser as well as the minister of information and culture and added a legal flavour to the government's decrees and proclamations. She vetted every bulletin issued. Hence, at the end of the day's work, she felt exhausted.

She summoned her energy and went to the dining table to take her lunch. She had never quite understood whether her eating at five o'clock was lunch or dinner. The snacks and bottles of coke she consumed in the office were really not meals.

She had become restless from not going outside the Presidential Mansion. She only left the grounds for official engagements during office hours. And that she did with an entourage that she knew included spies, who reported to the general. She would have liked to go out in her Baby Mercedes, the V-Boot of the elite class, and enjoy some fresh air, rather than be chauffeur-driven in a government car. She had not had the opportunity to go and thank those who had sent her congratulatory messages when she was appointed Minister of Information and Culture. The "Provost" of Akowe High School and Toyin Ajala had bought a page of *The Daily News* to congratulate her. That was a very kind gesture that she felt needed some type of reciprocation.

She was surprised though that her friend Ebi did not send her a card. Was she displeased with her acceptance of the ministerial appointment? What did she expect her to do after all that had happened to her? She was aware of the marriage fiasco. She had told her the experiences with both Architect Rube and Chief Ugbo.

She saw no reason why Ebi should be displeased with her. After all, she was offered the position freely, unlike others who lobbied hard and paid heavy cash for their appointments. She would like to meet Ebi in person and explain to her why she had chosen the side of the military. It was not an easy choice, but she had to seize the opportunity of this position of power to redeem her tarnished image from the smudges of poverty and divorce. She was sure that the stigma of divorce had vanished, washed off by her title, position, and connections. And thanks to her high military connections, she was no longer by any means a poor person. In the end, Ebi should understand her choice, which really was forced upon her by circumstances, she assured herself. It was not the contractors, those retired colonels, brigadiers, and generals who felt she owed them a contract because they had patronized her art shop that she wanted to see. She wanted to be out and to see how the National Art Company was faring, what was the current fashion for women on Allen Avenue, go to dance in nightclubs, and do many more things. She wanted to be like every woman, but she had become an imprisoned woman.

She had heard before her elevation to the ministerial position that her son, Uvie, was back in Lagos with Dede. She would like to see him. Would her son be proud of her? Would a time come that Uvie could spend time with her in the Presidential Mansion? No visitor was allowed to see her there for state security reasons. Her child, she believed, should be exempted from that rule. She would like to visit her mother at Arhagba in the Delta and see both her and her daughter Kena. She would have seized the opportunity of such a visit to pay a courtesy call on the Orodje of Okpe, who would be very pleased to meet one of his daughters in such a high cabinet position, but these had to be planned far ahead.

She had more than the wealth she had expected in her days of poverty or marriage. She had prayed for and sought wealth with a vengeance. She sent a good amount of money to her mother monthly to take care of herself and Kena. She also had fame. People now addressed her as Honourable Chief Franka Udi. How many women in the country were honourable or visible as she was as the minister of culture and information? She could think of none. She had really come a very long way from the days of her divorce to the present in which her face was a regular feature of the national television station.

Wealth and fame were not enough in life, she suddenly realized. Now she wanted to be ordinary and do simple things like visiting friends, attending ceremonies, and having her children around. She wanted friends around to chat over a wide range of things. She wanted to share in women's gossip. But now she was a social recluse.

As the president's mistress, really a concubine, and promised a wife's status, she had to censor herself. She was now Caesar's wife who must live above suspicion. She was experienced enough to know that General Ogiso was a very jealous man. What else could explain the banishing of Major-General Eugene Otu to Pakistan of all places? Besides, there was no telephone in her house in the Presidential Mansion complex. She had truly been transformed into a public figure that had no private life, except with the president.

She expected the general's promised confession to be nothing new. It was likely to be a reiteration of his love. Men, at the peak of lovemaking, become uncontrollable. They are capable of saying anything they feel that a woman would like to hear. Ogiso loved how she rolled him over to be on top of him. Other women had made love to him out of fear and had been tame in front of him, he had told her. She was like a rival general who wanted to defeat him with cunning. He had never experienced this before, and her body obsessed him. She had always wanted to be on top of men rather than beneath them, and now she had the opportunity to do so.

"You'll fit a First Lady so well," the general had told her.

"General, there's only one and whoever she is fits the position," she had said.

In private, she continued to address him as General; in the office he was "Mr. President." They tried to separate intimate from official dealings.

This general in particular had a flair for laying ambushes, she reflected. She did not want to be added to his harem. She enjoyed being more desired than the official wives who were never seen in public. They must be starving and why should she exchange her enviable position for theirs? She had stopped caring for the niceties of society, and it did not matter whether she was a concubine or girlfriend, but she did not want to be a wife. Perhaps, only if he agreed to abandon the other women! She had wanted to be a wife many years ago, but being a wife had not worked well for her. Even after her divorce, she still wanted to be a wife but all the men she met broke her heart and left her dejected. Now she believed that marriage worked for some people and did not work for others. She no longer wanted to be taunted with marriage by any man, president or general.

For days, whenever she asked him about the First Lady, the general had balked over the question and changed the subject. She, from her experience of married men, suspected he must be tired of her or having problems with her. She knew his public wife must be boring to him after she, Franka, had slept with him. How could that half-literate woman compete with her in bed or anywhere? What other woman knew how to have an orgasm three times in one sex act? What other woman would know how to treat a man so that he would go from orgasm to orgasm? Every other day was hers. She was happy that her share was the same or even more than that of the other women combined.

"There's no First Lady now," he told her.

"Where's she gone?" she asked.

"I can't tell, but she's no longer my wife," he answered.

"Don't play Henry VIII of England with me," she said, happy that her university education had made her very resourceful.

"Who's that Henry what?" he asked.

"Oh, I won't say, but he did a terrible thing to his wife," she said.

"And who did a terrible thing to her former husband?" he asked, taunting her.

He quickly realized this was a state secret that they should not talk about.

"Nothing can be terrible for a wicked and jealous woman," he said.

For almost six months, the First Lady had not appeared in public with the president. He had sent her to represent her on occasions. At first she had felt it was because of her position as minister of information and culture. But it now dawned on her that he was gradually phasing out the First Lady from public view. His intensifying passion for her was perplexing. When would he be sated? She had given him as much pleasure as she could invent, but he appeared to want more.

That night she went with the general for the first time to his living quarters nearby. If she slept in the general's bedroom, shared the executive bed with him, she would have exercised her own power over the most powerful man in the land. Men felt they wielded power, but women wielded their own power over them, she contemplated.

The bedroom, as would be expected, was beyond description in its glamour. The huge gold-coated bed bigger than a king size dazzled her. She always knew that since her own bedroom was so plush and comfortable, the general's would be beyond comparison of any other in the land. She wondered whether such a bed would make you sleep more soundly than ordinary beds. The sheets were so silky and comfortable. The air-conditioners were murmuring and blowing out very cold air. There was a two-seater lazy-boy on the side. The general sat her there and himself after her. The gold and the mirrors overwhelmed her and as soon as he held her hand and fondled her breasts, the sensation caused her to have an orgasm. She felt it was wasted. She wished she had held it back for later.

Without being asked by the general, she removed her shoes and started to change into her nightgown, the special lingerie that then Brigadier Otu had picked for her from Marks & Spencer. Eugene Otu never saw her in it. She wanted something special today, hence she wore it. She was no longer an innocent woman and she knew what she had been brought there for.

The general removed his charm from his neck. He normally did not wear it when he came to meet her at hers. He also began to undress. She had never asked him about the scars and marks on his chest. They were not birthmarks and must be incisions of the medicine men that prepared traditional medicines for him to overcome his enemies and evil spirits. There were questions you did not ask an adult, and she felt she did not need to pry too much into the general's private life.

When she woke in the morning, the general was not snoring as he did whenever they slept together. At first she felt he had exhausted himself. After all, it had been a busy night for both of them. When she looked closer in his side of the bed, she was amazed to see him hunched up. When she stretched her hand to tickle him as she did when she woke before him, she plunged into a nightmare. This could not be real! The body beside her was still and cold. She tried to shake him but there was no movement from him. The body was cold and stone heavy.

She wanted to shout, but instinctively stifled the shout. How would she shout that the general, the president of the Federal Republic and Commander-in-Chief of the Armed Forces, who brought her to sleep with him was dead? What was she doing there in the first place? The country and the world would surely hold her responsible for the president's death. She would be accused of poisoning him. What else could have killed the leopard that was so full of energy? How could the python be still? What brought the elephant down? How come the tortoise was lying on its back?

"Only God can handle this!" she exclaimed to herself.

She climbed down from the bed to say "Hail Mary", but she could not complete it. It had been too many years since she had gone to Mass. She knew this was not what any saint or Holy Mother could solve for her. She had to think fast about what to do.

She stared at the general's body on the bed for over a half-hour because she didn't know what to do next. Was this not the man who was so thrilled last night with love that he had sung military songs as she was on top of him? Was this not the man who had shouted meaningless praises to her in his joy? Was this not the man she had praised last night for holding his orgasm until she was ready, and this was done three times?

She covered the body with a bedspread and locked the bedroom door and, with the key in her handbag, went to her own quarters to get ready for the day's work.

It was Thursday, September 30, the day before Independence Day; the day before the week of national mourning was to begin. The appearance of normalcy had to be maintained, she decided. Things had always been that way and had to continue to be so. The major problem was how to deal with the president's broadcast scheduled for the evening of Independence Day.

Now she brought into use her study of English at a crucial moment. What was unfolding was like the tales of fiction. No wonder Ian Watt defined the novel as an imagined story that reflects life. Life is fiction and fiction life, she now realized.

As she drove to her office just outside the Presidential Mansion complex that Thursday morning, ideas ran wild in her head. She had heard of the Jukun practice in which the dead Aku Uka, dressed in royal regalia, paraded the streets of Wukari on horseback, as if he were still alive. Could this be done for General Ogiso, to inspect the guard of honour at the Heroes' Arcade at the Tafawa Balewa Square? For security reasons, the president's formal activities on Independence Day had not been announced. It would be a coup of a special kind if the general's body was prepared like the Aku Uka but in his ceremonial dress and rode a horse to and from the parade ground. General Ogiso liked to confuse the entire nation about his movements. Most times, the people learned about what the president had done through the television and radio. Many sceptics believed that the president's own security detail comprised photographers and journalists and he did not need to leave his office or home to be reported as having performed many activities. In this tradition, she believed that she could stage-manage something realistic that would not raise any suspicion about the president's condition.

She also knew the practice common in Edo areas of not announcing the monarch's death until six months after. Meanwhile the chiefs issued riddling statements to describe the state of the kingdom. When the last Okpe king died, the chiefs announced that the tree had entered the river! There was also a statement that the sky had lost its support. The sky will not fall because it loses its support, just as a country lives on after the death of its president. Could she run the Federal Republic like a powerful Benin senior chief? She would issue a proclamation: the leopard has at last gone to sleep! The cock has crowed its last dawn! The cat has slipped into the forest! The tortoise has burst out of its own shell!

After all, she was an Okpe chief and her people had the same traditions as in Benin. Could she prevail on an inner circle and run the Federal Government for six months or more, while giving the appearance of executing General Ogiso's orders? Or could she do the ruling alone? She considered most people in uniform, officers and men, as zombies. At best they were robots. They carried out orders without questioning. Within the six months, she could dismiss and eliminate officers she was not comfortable with. The overzealous Chief Ofe (now posted as a colonel commanding the Presidential Bodyguard) could be promoted to the rank of major-general and made the new chief of army staff. In another six months when the death would be announced, so many skulls would have been raised from the army hierarchy itself to cushion the general's body in the grave. There were many precedents of such happenings.

With a variety of ideas bubbling in her mind, she started work immediately. One of the few things she had learned in government was to keep the airwaves busy with pronouncements. The papers would pick them up by their next publication.

The airwaves must be saturated with announcements. The populace would easily be deceived into believing that the government was busy in its task of governance. She issued a special bulletin in the president's fashion to be broadcast immediately. She was used to these things now as she had written many for the government since joining the cabinet. What a degree in English can do in times like this! She exclaimed to herself.

IT HAS COME TO GOVERNMENT ATTENTION THAT EVERY ASSOCIATION OR ORGANIZATION HAS A SO-CALLED PRESIDENT. THE FEDERAL MILITARY GOVERNMENT CANNOT LOOK ON AND WATCH THE SACRED NAME OF THE PRESIDENT DEFILED AND ABUSED BY POWER-HUNGRY PERSONS. THERE CAN BE ONLY ONE PRESIDENT IN A REPUBLIC AND THIS NATION HAS ONLY ONE. HENCEFORTH THOSE WHO HEAD SUCH GROUPS SHOULD CALL THEMSELVES BY OTHER NAMES SUCH AS CHAIRMAN OR CO-ORDINATOR. MY GOVERNMENT IS TIRED OF HEARING ABOUT THESE PEOPLE DAYDREAMING ABOUT THE PRESIDENCY. THOSE WHO VIOLATE THIS ORDER WILL RECEIVE THE HARSHEST PUNISHMENT FROM THE EXECUTIVE BRANCH OF GOVERNMENT. I REMAIN THE PRESIDENT OF THE FEDERAL REPUBLIC. LONG LIVE THE PRESIDENCY!
SIGNED: THE PRESIDENT.

A dispatcher took it by hand to the radio and television, which immediately interrupted the regular program to air the message.

She scheduled two other special bulletins for afternoon and evening respectively. The afternoon bulletin, for some rather mysterious reasons, dealt with women.

TO ENCOURAGE ALL WOMEN TO FULLY REALIZE THE BENEFITS OF THEIR WOMANHOOD AND FOR THEIR HUSBANDS TO BE RESPONSIBLE, NO WOMAN IN THIS COUNTRY SHOULD HENCEFORTH BE CIRCUMCIZED IN COMPLIANCE WITH THE WORLD HEALTH ORGANIZATION'S UNIVERSAL DECLARATION. OUR DEAR COUNTRY IS A RESPONSIBLE MEMBER OF THE WORLD BODY. THE PRACTICE OF FEMALE CIRCUMCISION OR EXCISION IS BANNED WITH IMMEDIATE EFFECT. PARENTS WILL BE HELD RESPONSIBLE SHOULD THEY VIOLATE THE LAW.

She had always felt lucky that she was not circumcised when she was young. The death of three girls in the family from circumcision had made her parents resolve not to have her go through the ritual. Two had bled helplessly to death and one suffered an infection that locked her jaws and life forever. She had delivered her children without being circumcised and she had felt very good about her body. She hoped this order would be heeded. After all, she had risen to where she was because she was an uncircumcised woman.

The final bulletin in the president's name that appeared on the evening that preceded the scheduled national broadcast took a different direction from the earlier two.

ALL TRADITIONAL RULERS SHOULD STAND PREPARED TO TAKE OVER ADMINISTRATION OF THEIR LOCAL GOVERNMENTS. THEY SHOULD ALSO STAND PREPARED TO ACCEPT RESPONSIBILITY OF VIOLATIONS OF STATE LAWS BY THEIR OWN PEOPLE. EVERYBODY MUST BE VIGILANT TO CATCH LAW-BREAKERS. THE NET IS CAST TO FISH OUT THE SHARKS FROM OUR WATERS!

Before she closed from work, she had to speak as Minister of Information and Culture. Her ministry put out the information, which was broadcast immediately, that the president's live national day broadcast had been postponed. She left the postponement vague until she could think of how best to fill in the future with the illusion of normalcy. All citizens should wait for further announcements from the ministry on when the broadcast would take place. Since the postponement of broadcasts was a common practice of President Ogiso, nobody suspected anything was wrong.

By the time she left her office that evening, she felt good that she had managed the day and the nation very well. She believed that all along what the president did was to manage the nation day by day because the cabinet discussed matters arising all the time. They often discussed how to beef up security, how to suppress imagined insurrections, and how to eliminate government critics. They did not discuss or debate a plan for the country, and no member of the cabinet suggested anything else to be done.

27

"As I have told you the past few days, your daughter will get better day by day," Dr. Lateef Laoye explained to Dede and Furu.

He had called them to his office to talk to them. Already he had signed Tetebe's discharge authorization and he wanted to assure his patient's parents about her prospects. In his many years as a doctor of children, he believed in explaining as much as possible to parents, because the more they understood their sick children's conditions the better they would deal with their personal stresses and their children's health.

"Transfusion has done your daughter good, but, hopefully, after several transfusions, she will not need to have more," he continued. "Transfusion should boost her blood count and raise the white blood corpuscles for some time. The sickling process would begin almost immediately, but, all things being equal, it should take a long time before it came to the point when she would need another transfusion. Like every drastic measure, blood transfusion has its positive and negative effects. Luckily, from our tests, her iron has not risen above the normal level for children. With time, we have to watch out for that. Too much iron is not good for her liver and kidneys. If iron poses a problem, it has to be painfully removed. Desferol or deferoxamine is the best known medication for that. It is given with a needle several times a week, depending on the amount of iron in the blood. And you cannot trust any blood used for transfusion one hundred percent because some vials could carry infections or antibodies. There is always the danger of HIV and hepatitis, if the blood is not carefully screened. I don't expect these bad things, but it is my responsibility to tell you," Dr.

Laoye said.

"Thank you," Dede and Furu replied.

"One more thing," the doctor continued. "Don't be unnecessarily anxious. The treatment of sickle cell disease will continue to improve and there are signs in medical research that an effective drug will be ready for use in the near future. Medical researchers are also looking at bone marrow transplant. For now, before the researchers produce a cure or an effective-control drug, follow the management procedures in *The Handbook* that I gave you. All will be well."

They were grateful for Dr. Laoye's concern and encouragement. A good doctor, he was their counsellor who had calmed their nerves. They could swear before any skeptics that there was a serious-minded doctor, who did not fit the stereotype of the moneymaking, unconcerned doctors in the country. Dr. Laoye was an exceptionally dedicated doctor.

The two parents felt relieved. The future would surely be brighter than the present, difficult time they were experiencing. If Tetebe could survive the pains and anguish of the crises, a time would come when she would not suffer anymore. They were hoping for a pain-free future.

They left the doctor's office, and walked to the ward to take Tetebe home. They called a nurse to cut off the plastic band of identification from her right wrist. Dede took the band and threw it into a trash bucket by the corner of the room.

Furu folded the clothes as Dede left for the general waiting room where Uvie was waiting, half-asleep.

"Tete," Furu called her daughter, "we'll soon go home and you'll have the whole house to play in."

"Can I ride my bike to school?" Tetebe asked.

"Not in Lagos. Daddy will take you there in his car," Furu explained.

"When will you have your own car?" she asked.

"When we have more money," Furu answered.

"Will I drive the car?"

"Yes, when you grow up and have a driver's license."

Dede and Uvie came in. Uvie rushed to hold Tetebe's hand. The two children ran out of the room into the corridor ahead of their parents. They ran back when they saw Dr. Laoye coming towards them.

As Dede and Furu lifted the bags from the ground to leave, the doctor came in.

"Mr. Daro, take good care of yourself; these must be very hard times for both of you in every way, but you'll be all right," he counselled.

"Thank you for all you have done for us," Dede told him.

"We are grateful," Furu said.

"It's been a pleasure," Dr. Laoye replied.

When they were at the hospital gate, Dede suddenly remembered that he had to go to a meeting of the executive committee of the National Forum for Democracy. It was Thursday, a key day in the preparation for the week of national mourning, which would begin the following day. The nation was also expecting President Ogiso's Independence Day broadcast the same day, however delayed.

Though he was relieved that Tetebe was now well, Dede was anxious over the new responsibilities. He wanted to participate actively in the ongoing events. The thought of cocks, hens, and young ones not fleeing and together catching the hawk to account for its many earlier crimes of kidnapping and murder, came to his mind.

At the same time that he was engrossed in the national situation, he wanted to be close to Tetebe, Uvie, and Furu. He felt he needed to be with them. This was a special moment for them. Tetebe had recovered and was in good spirits and Uvie had gradually fully integrated into the family. They were now truly one strong family. His thoughts also went to Kena and his own parents, all of whom he had not seen in recent months. He barely had time to do what he needed to do, he felt.

28

It was after office hours that Thursday that Franka's real task of covering up began. The following day, the much-anticipated national day, was a public holiday. It would be a work-free day but she hoped to work hard on the emergency on her hands. It would be a serious test of her ability to manage the nation as a proxy president. If she had been busy in the office, she had to be busier at home. The clock was ticking and she knew that she had begun living a proxy life for General Ogiso. She was no longer just herself. She was even not just President Ogiso. She was already the nation.

She did not feel hungry. She changed from her office dress into a less formal traditional gown. She reflected for a moment on how the previous night, without wearing a bra or any other underwear, she had gone to the general's bedchamber. The general had experienced the best sex of his life. They were both exhausted from the wild sex, especially as the third round had culminated in a simultaneous cry that had left both of them silent until she woke up from her reverie and made the frightening discovery. It was a crazy act that had resulted in a strange situation in which she now had to keep the dead alive in the mind of the public.

She mustered courage and walked to the general's quarters. There was nothing unusual in that, she felt. She took the key from her handbag, opened the front door, and inserted the key into the bedroom door with some anxiety. She hoped for a miracle to solve her big problem. After turning the key, she gradually pushed back the door and looked as if she expected to greet and hug a revived lover. The bed was as she had left it in the morning, neatly arranged, and with a bedspread over the body. The air-conditioners were wheezing, the bedroom very cold.

That night, alone with the general's body, she behaved like a soldier in battle, flanked by corpses. Her own survival counted more than the dead beside her. After staring for several minutes at the bed, she was troubled by the cold air in the room that began to numb her senses. There was always light in the Presidential Mansion as the national electric power agency made sure that it worked non-stop. Despite that assurance, another high-voltage generator stood by to kick off in case of an unexpected interruption, to be doubly sure that there was always light in the Presidential Mansion complex. She went to turn off all three air-conditioners in the bedroom. She soon became scared of the silence in the room and went back to start two of the air-conditioners.

Whenever she came back from work, she used to be lonely until the general called. Now still beside her, she felt the silence crushing her. She went to the other side of the bedroom where the two-seater lazy-boy was and fell into it. She wanted to turn on the television, a special one with countless channels, but put off the idea of watching television. This was not the time to waste in watching news or entertainment programs, with the serious life-and-death issues that needed to be solved. Rather, she tried to imagine how she could get out of the net in which she found herself trapped. Her greatest shield and weapon had been the body on the bed. She could not think of an immediate way to get out, short of the body coming back to life.

She wished that God would work a miracle for her by bringing the general back to life. She knew she was a sinner, but she pleaded for God's grace. "Our father who art in heaven," she started. Soon she was distracted from the prayer by the shadow of the body reflecting from a combination of gold and mirrors around her. Not mirrors, but the huge mirror. Why did the president have this mirror in his bedroom? Why would people want to watch themselves in bed in the mirror? A stutter by the air-conditioner drew her attention back to the body on the big bed. When she was in secondary school, her history teacher had always complained that her attention could not remain fixed on one thing for a few seconds. She had felt he had a knack for hyperbole and so exaggerated her condition. She was much grown up now but had not shed that feature entirely.

She felt she would follow a tested line of action to save the situation for the time being. She would continue to issue more bulletins or public announcements to stay busy. The president used to give the impression that he did not sleep most nights because he was attending to state matters. Coming to her at night was one of the president's state matters! He came to the office at twelve noon and kept his cabinet ministers and foreign visitors waiting to see him. He had no sense of keeping appointments and ran the government like a private estate. Now she had to watch through the night the burden of state.

She cast a long look at the general limp on the bed. She sprinkled her most provocative French perfume on the bedspread covering the body. It is possible that the powerful, even in death, could be deodorized to smell good, she felt. After this ritual, she decided to go back to her own quarters.

When the clock on her bedroom wall struck midnight, she suddenly developed an empty feeling. It was now Independence Day. Her stomach became hollow, her head dizzy. She was confused about where she was. Sweat beads sprang over her body. She thought it was a sensation of hunger because she had not eaten for twelve hours or so. She went to her refrigerator and took some slices of bread, which she laced lavishly with margarine to eat. She poured water from the flask for a cup of hot chocolate with milk.

With the cup of chocolate in hand, she went to get her pen. She made up her mind that the first bulletin in the morning on Independence Day would announce another postponement of the expected broadcast. After all, the country's life as an independent state had always been a postponement of national realizations. So many dreams continued to be deferred. A nation that held the prospect of greatness languished in poverty, corruption, and tyranny. A nation rich in human and natural resources was now counted among the poorest on the planet. She, Franka, was only an agent of both President Ogiso and fate to further confuse the state. She had been a schemer, an experienced one at that, but the ongoing happenings were thrust upon her by chance. In her ruminations, she kicked a stool and stumbled. The cup of chocolate fell from her hand and splashed on the floor. She soon collected herself, got a mop to clean the terrazzo floor. In the meantime some ideas came to her mind. She went to sit by her dining table, and set out to write.

THE PRESIDENT'S BROADCAST IS HEREBY POSTPONED. KEEP TUNED FOR DEVELOPMENTS.

She liked her dining table, but nobody except the general had sat there with her. What was the use of having a beautifully furnished house, if people did not visit you to admire it and compliment you? She would have liked guests to praise her house and furniture, but she had only one guest and he was gone. She knew her mind was wandering again at a crucial time that she must act fast to solve her problem, which was also the nation's problem.

Though Friday was a public holiday, she would take the sheet of handwritten paper to the television station and read it herself. Her mind went to the crazy military boys who had seized radio and television stations many years back to announce a take-over that failed and they had received the ultimate punishment of coup plotters: death by firing squad! Failure always brings one down, she realized. In any case, one did not need to be in uniform to take over the government, she felt. Anybody with courage can take over the administration of this country. Would she be the first woman to seize power in the country? She tried to refocus her mind on the dilemma at hand.

She thought of reading the bulletin at 7 a.m., the very moment the people, despite their complaints against the government, listened to the first network news of the day and would therefore glue their ears to the radio and their eyes to the television screen. She might even tickle them with the national anthem before reading the announcement. President Ogiso's friendly opening was well known: "My fellow citizens!" This was better than the "Fellow countrymen!" that he used to start his broadcasts with. Why "countrymen" and "compatriots," as if all the people of this nation were male? Why not address "countrywomen" and "matriots"? she asked herself.

She succumbed to the temptation of writing and reading the broadcast on behalf of President Ogiso. Those broadcasts started with a summation of imaginary achievements and dreams for the future. If these reviews were right, the country would now have been in the company of at least Brazil, India, Malaysia, Singapore, and South Korea, if not that of Britain, France, and the United States. There had to be some threats against lawlessness in the statement: "The firm arm of the law will catch up with those who attempt to disrupt my government."

She set the alarm for six o'clock and woke early. She felt light. Everything around her appeared strange. She hurriedly took a shower and dressed in her most formal traditional gown. She did what she had planned to do—drive to the television station not too far away. The soldiers on guard gave her the salute and passed her. Her serious demeanour confused the Duty Manager of the National Television Authority who, of course, gave her access to make her broadcast. After all, she was the cabinet member responsible for the national media houses.

After a lady announcer said there would be a special announcement, she took over. She introduced herself as Chief Franka Udi, the Minister of Information and Culture, as if she was not known by the public, and said that she had a statement for the nation. Even as she read it, her mind wandered into many possibilities. Couldn't she be the first female civilian to overthrow a military government in Africa? After all, she could announce taking over power and dismiss all the officers she did not like. She knew once the officers heard that there was a coup, they would hide themselves and be ready to pledge support or loyalty to the new commander-in-chief. She knew she could use some of the officers and so should dismiss those that she felt would resist her rule. Power was already in her hands. She suddenly realized that her mind had wandered into a dangerous zone and she needed to retreat into the important matter of the moment. The price of a failed coup was public execution.

She needed to say something creative to grab the attention of the nation. On the spur of the moment, she continued.

ANOTHER BULLETIN. THE BAN ON PRIVATE NEWSPAPERS IS HEREBY LIFTED BY GOVERNMENT WITH IMMEDIATE EFFECT. EDITORS SHOULD EXERCISE MAXIMUM RESTRAINT FOR NATIONAL INTEREST. IT IS MY GOVERNMENT'S POLICY TO ENCOURAGE FREE SPEECH AND DEMOCRATIC PRINCIPLES.

After this, she told viewers that the president's speech would be read "later in the day. Stay tuned."

The people tried to second-guess the military president's activities at the time. He was busy attending to some urgent matters before addressing the nation. Was he not busy preparing his speech, which, like everything he did, was delayed? There had been rumours promoted by his supporters several years ago that the president often sought solitude, as the Osagyefo of Ghana, Dr. Kwame Nkrumah, did so as to meditate on delicate national issues before taking a decision. Was he now communing with gods, stars, and totemic animals for a broadcast to change the sinking fortune of his regime? If he had gone on a one-man retreat to meditate on the affairs of state, was he, during his public silence, telephoning the angels for what to say? Did he climb any mountain that he would descend with a new vision for the country?

She came out of the television station only to see demonstrators already trickling into the city centre to move towards the National Secretariat.

At their late night meeting, the executive committees of labour unions, the NAFORD, the NAD, and other human rights groups opted to seize the people's secretariat rather than to march in protest in front of the Presidential Mansion. They reasoned that isolating the leadership would further erode its power and unite the people in a patriotic manner. The leaders of the democratic coalitions ruled against a frontal attack to avoid shedding the blood of innocent people. They knew that

President Ogiso's forces would not hesitate to fire at the crowd of marchers. The fierce-looking leader would not mind wiping out the entire population of the country in the name of maintaining national security to ensure peace and stability. From the pronouncements coming out, national security had become the junta's excuse to do whatever it liked. It was needless to provoke the leopard by thrusting your hand into its mouth! It would be a fatal mistake to test the cobra's bite in response to a provocation. The protest leaders were thoughtful people and they wanted to protect their followers. In the city centre, the earliest people to come out boldly to protest were the disabled. It appeared as if most workers had stayed at home for fear of being shot. The atmosphere of apparent fear intensified as army and police vans of heavily armed convoys drove past the main streets. In combat fatigues and wearing helmets, they looked wild and hungry for blood. A few tanks stood at major intersections of the city. The Ministers of Defence and Internal Affairs were coordinating the movement of troops to deal with the situation. That was what President Ogiso expected of them, they believed. They thought and planned with the general's mind.

The situation was tense and the public feared a blood bath as had happened on several occasions in the past. The people suspected the President would unleash his savage power against the demonstrators. Why, they asked themselves, had he not made his national day broadcast? He was unpredictable in his tactics but his means were always brutal. Was he not the one who publicly boasted that if he had to kill over half the nation to stay in power as the longest-ruling president in Africa, he would do it? He had been able to visit only Liberia and Zaire for the past seven years and he had learned a lot from his colleagues in Monrovia and Kinshasa.

As she left the television station for her Presidential Mansion home, Franka's feelings changed from hot to cold and back and forth. It appeared a strong wind was blowing inside her. She saw the disabled, whom she had disparagingly called Dede's phantom militia at a cabinet meeting. She believed that Dede would use them to embarrass the government. She was now the government. Where were the other protesters that the cabinet had been working day and night to keep away from coming out, but who vowed they would definitely come out? It appeared to her that the problem was not as bad as anticipated. She could order the Commander of the National Guard to wipe out the demonstrators from the street, but how would that decision and action help her to keep General Ogiso's death a secret and allow her to rule in his name for as long as she liked?

The presence of General Ogiso's official but rarely seen wives and the Chief of Army Staff in front of the general's house made her panic. Before she drew near her own bungalow, her head was hot and she forgot the elaborate plan that she had been working on to keep everybody in the dark about the general's death. They beckoned her, and when she did not show any sign of quick response to the call, the Chief of Army Staff yelled out her name. She could not pretend that she did not hear the call.

She went to them, greeted them, and asked whether there was a problem. She had taken several courses in drama in her undergraduate years, and she knew that she had to put on an air of composure to appear innocent. And that she tried to do well. However, the way the president's wives looked at her frightened her and she knew that she was no longer safe in the presidential complex. They told her the president had not been seen for prayers for a full day, which was unusual.

"The servants confirmed that he had not come to eat since yesterday," said Major-General Daudu, the Chief of Army Staff.

The dining room was a hallway outside the President's own house. He usually walked in to eat but occasionally missed some meals. The cooks were always ready for breakfast, lunch, or dinner.

"Even when he wanted to be alone or think about state matters, he would come out, past my place, once a day. He never failed to be in my room," the senior wife said.

Dr. Hajia, who used to be paraded as First Lady with her coquettish headdress and smile, was not there.

"He used to leave the bedroom door open, but now it is locked," said the junior wife, who had peeped in and seen the door not ajar but closed.

"He did not come to me last night as he used to," she continued.

Franka wondered how the general was able to meet the demands of all of them. She had been mistaken about his capability to see all his wives and herself. The man was definitely stronger than she had given him credit for. She had thought that, since her divorce, she alone was more than enough for one man to cope with. But this was not the time for such frivolous thoughts.

"We had a meeting of the intelligence branch and he did not show up," Major-General Daudu added.

"He must be in," Franka said, "or relaxing in one of his guest houses."

"He still has to make his live nationwide broadcast to the people of this country," Major-General Daudu again said.

"He must be preparing to address the nation now," she said.

She knew she did not have much time to be in this hostile environment. There was a limit to what problems play-acting could save her from. She needed more than play-acting to survive the current dilemma. The Chief of Army Staff had not had free access to General Ogiso for some time and he must be blaming her as responsible. He took it as a form of humiliation and downgrading to be kept away from the president's ears. And the president's wives knew all along her relationship with their husband. If they had had access to poison her, they certainly would have done so. She felt she had to flee for her life's sake. These faces had so much hatred in them that they could stone her to death, if given the chance.

The minister went back to her house and quickly packed a few of her most important belongings in a suitcase. She shoved another big suitcase filled with fifty naira notes out of one of the closets. She put the two suitcases in the car boot and drove off. She realized that it would be a matter of minutes before the president's death would be known.

Chief Franka Udi had not conceded that she could not handle the entire nation and also the state executive's body anymore. She had only made a tactical retreat from the Presidential Mansion because she felt exposed there. She drove to the television station to issue more special announcements. She discovered that she had not thought of any new decrees and so asked the announcer to re-read what she had read earlier in the day.

By the time she felt she was not safe in the television grounds either, she went back to her car to drive to her house in town. But she no longer held the keys to her own house in Victoria Island and would have to find out from the Director of State Intelligence. And that agency in particular had been sorely treated and was still smarting over what its members considered her hijacking of the president into her bosom, where she controlled him. Once they knew what had happened, they would deal with her in a severe manner. She had even blocked a vote for the agency in a cabinet meeting, saying such a huge amount was not needed. The agency got to know who cut their budget and threw their big slice of the national cake away. She had nowhere she could think of to go. She had instantly become homeless in Lagos!

The atmosphere had changed within the hour. The streets were astir with suspense as the demonstrators were already marching. Many more people were coming out, undeterred by the military's known brutal tactics in suppressing peaceful demonstrations that they called riots. As others saw people coming out, they also joined and the crowd became a swell of the population. Lagos was on its feet, moving.

Meanwhile, at the Presidential Mansion, they had broken into the bedroom and discovered the president's body. Major-General Daudu had asked for Chief Franka Udi to be called and, when told she had driven out, asked for her apprehension.

The wails of the general's wives and servers had reached the ears of those who were asking questions about the president and his expected Independence Day broadcast. Within minutes telephones were ringing with callers asking questions as to whether what they had just heard was true or not. Nobody was bold enough yet to pronounce the unpronounceable. Can the king of the sky die? Could this be a ruse to round up people later as coup plotters for execution? There was nothing that the president could not do in the name of national security. He could put out word of his own death to see how people would respond and then ask his agents to round up those who showed signs of jubilation for plotting to kill him. Their end would be public execution in order to deter other citizens of the country from thinking ill of the president.

The protesters stopped her in front of *The African Patriot*. She had been dazed and did not know where to go but had to keep on driving. She was surrounded and knew she was going to be neck-laced. Theirs was a consumer nation and people imported the most recent gadgets, cars, and clothes, as well as the habits of other people from other countries. They had borrowed the South African practice of putting a tire round a traitor's neck and using it to set the person ablaze.

"I am Mrs. Daro," she shouted.

"No, this is not Mrs. Daro. She is Honourable Chief Franka Udi, Minister of Information and Culture," someone corrected her.

They dragged her out of her Mercedes Benz car. She looked terrified as a condemned robber facing a firing squad in one of the Bar Beach shows that the military junta used to entertain the common people.

As a group of demonstrators shouted her easily identifiable name, Chief Franka Udi, Dede appeared from among the crowd that easily recognized the renowned journalist. He had seen her from a distance and, knowing she was in danger, shoved his way through to reach her. He arrived by her side almost breathless. He cleared some space for her to be left alone. He told the protesters around that news was coming in about the death of the president in his sleep and that they should march toward the Presidential Mansion. With excitement, they left her and surged towards the Presidential Mansion.

She felt grateful and ashamed at the same time. Dede and she had been divorced for six years or so and since then so much had happened to her and also to him. She had witnessed the proscribed lecture at the University of Lagos. She got a security report when the NAD was formed. She was sorry for the decision about the parcel bomb that a special security committee approved. It was a collective decision and she could not have said no to it. All the other members had known that her former husband was the thorn in the flesh of the Ogiso Administration. But fortunately he was alive and had saved her life. She had broken away from him and gone to every length possible in the land to impress, humiliate, or even destroy him. He was not only very lucky to be alive but also possessed a resilience of spirit that defied the diabolical schemes of the president, she thought.

Now, as he stood before her, she was the proverbial person running away from death only to find death squatting in front of her in her so-called refuge. She had wanted him to be disabled but not killed so that she could laugh at him. However, state actions were taken in the president's interest and not the cabinet's. She could not now ask how he had managed to escape being hurt or killed by the bomb. In her mind, she thought the person who had survived that explosion must have a charmed life. From her eyes, Dede believed she knew that he also knew the role she had played in the parcel bomb incident.

"Don't go to your house yet. Go to your friend Ebi's place. You'll be safe there. Things will cool down and you'll be all right," he told her.

"I've not seen her for many years," she replied.

"She still lives where she used to. Go there and stay out of the public's eye for your own safety," he emphasized.

"How are the children?" she asked.

"Fine. Uvie is here and doing fine," he answered.

They stared at each other.

"You must leave for Ebi's place right away," he told her.

As she ran for her dear life through the crowd, some people who knew her as the Minister of Information and Culture set her Baby Mercedes Benz ablaze to sate their rage. She remembered the two suitcases in the boot of the car but quickly realized that she had to either save her life or sacrifice her wealth and herself together. The choice was not difficult to make.

The African Patriot came out the following morning. The lifting of the ban on independent newspapers was quickly followed by production. All the editors had been standing by for the time to re-start production. The machines were serviced and waiting for work all the while. It was therefore easy to roll out the first post-Ogiso issue of the paper. It told the story of what had happened the previous day, with photographs of soldiers throwing away their guns and military uniform so as not to be lynched by the crowd. Many of the soldiers took up the green leaves that the people had brandished as a sign of their new freedom. There were the photos of the crowd and Franka's flaming car, the only case of arson in what the paper described as a peaceful revolution.

The government was without a leader, but nobody wanted to be the head without the authority of the people. Several ambitious army officers briefly contemplated stepping into the void created to assert leadership, but when they saw the huge crowd they restrained themselves. All the people in the nation's capital appeared to be out in the streets. The officers knew that whoever seized power for selfish ends would have no peace. Even the army upstarts now believed that authority had to be earned from the people. By the following day, when General Ogiso was buried, he was treated like a vulture. A few of his kind wept for him but the Ogiso tyranny had come to an end. An interim administration was established to run the affairs of the country and conduct free elections. It consisted of three military officers that were known to be hostile to General Ogiso and six civilians. The chairmanship would rotate alphabetically for the nine months they would rule before the general elections. There was also an advisory committee to the interim government and Dede Daro was one of the twenty-one persons not only appointed to monitor and advise but also to ensure that the provisional administration fulfilled the people's hopes for freedom, democracy, and prosperity.

At home Dede and Furu celebrated the change they had hoped for but had not thought would happen so soon. Tetebe was fine and hilarious. She did not understand national politics but felt something festive was taking place; she was happy at her parents' outpouring of joy. Uvie knew that there was a change of government and did not quite know what to make of the whole euphoria. He now felt very much at home in Lagos and did not seem to miss his grandparents and Okpara too much any longer.

Dede wrote a poem about cutting off the cobra's tail, which he hoped to publish in the Sunday edition of his paper. The poem was both a warning against making mistakes of the past and a reminder that the new leaders would have to prove themselves worthy of their responsibilities.

Epilogue: Spoken by the Chorus

We have cut the cobra's tail
and now rejoice at striking a death blow.
We shower tears to celebrate or grieve:
we can only ask for more of the salt of smiles
and not for none of that of agonizing pain.
We have shed blood for peace,
had love savaged by beastly wiles.
Perhaps we cannot come out as total victors;
we win mock battles to swell our heads.
When a flash storm gathers tyrannical strength,
it breaks the only tall palm tree of the land.
Politics and the military are breeding grounds
for a summit of torturers.
We have cut the cobra's tail
and the land must rest from its raids.
May it not re-appear with a more poisonous tail!

The papers overflowed with headlines and special reports. *The Lagos Weekend* unexpectedly came closest to the truth that was buried in Franka's heart.

PRESIDENT DIED OF HEART FAILURE ON TOP OF HIS MINISTER

The long rule of General Ogiso came to an abrupt but pleasant end when he collapsed on top of his minister mistress and died immediately. He apparently fell victim to the *magun* medicine that her former husband had prepared to curb her flirtatious life when they were husband and wife six years ago. The former husband had already invited people to a party even before the general's death came to light. ..

In a separate article titled DICTATOR KILLED BY LOVER, another reporter wrote of the former president's lover poisoning his drink with arsenic that she had secured from a new lover in the army. The general had failed to heed the warnings of his diviners to stop his affair with the woman and expel her from the Presidential Mansion grounds. Quoting several wives of the late dictator, the paper said that one of his experienced *marabous* had consistently demanded the expulsion of the woman minister, but that she had cast such a strong spell on him the relationship continued till the devil caught up with him.

There was a third piece titled: CHIEF FRANKA UDI FREES THE

NATION FROM TYRANNY.

Quoting what he described as anonymous but reliable sources, the correspondent wrote that both Dede Daro of *The African Patriot* and the former minister of information and culture, Chief Franka Udi, worked in unison to bring down General Ogiso. The writer went on to remind the public that he felt had a short memory that these two people had once been husband and wife. He recollected vividly their divorce and child custody cases and how they had at that time brought notoriety and infamy to their persons and to the marriage institution. Now, as if speaking for his readers, he absolved them and proclaimed them national heroes.

Dede now discovered that life itself was fiction, which did not need to be imagined but observed and recorded. He had wanted to write fiction, which was always available, but felt pleased with his poetry. He was looking forward to which writer would win the story contest of the weekend papers at year's end. There were so many stories to pick a winner from.

When Franka, now at Ebi's, read the papers, she felt she did not need to live in hiding for the rest of her life. She had expected that only the anonymity of night would take her out to have fresh air. But with that type of reporting in the weekend papers, she would be safe to have a second chance to live a good life in the open. She was pleased so far that she had not been summoned to say what she knew about the late dictator's end. Nobody really cared about the death of a vulture. It infected the earth with rot.

She knew she would go back to her Victoria Beach house in a matter of days. However, she wondered how she would get back her Art Shop that had been transformed. Her staggering bank account was intact and she would not suffer from want for the rest of her life. All she had set out to do with money and men was to live comfortably. Also, she had to fill a void that had taken over her life after the divorce. But life was far more complicated than she had thought. If in that endeavour to live well and fill a void she had unwittingly removed a dictator, fine. Her private interests had served the public good. She wondered though what Dede would think of the whole situation and especially of the correspondent who had named them liberators and heroes.